THE SEA BELOW MY WINDOW

Everything is present.

OLE SARVIG

THE SEA
BELOW MY WINDOW

*Translated from the Danish
by Anni Whissen*

*

MASTERWORKS OF FICTION (1960)

GREEN INTEGER
KØBENHAVN *&* LOS ANGELES
2003

GREEN INTEGER BOOKS
Edited by Per Bregne
København/Los Angeles

Distributed in the United States by Consortium Book
Sales and Distribution, 1045 Westgate Drive, Suite 90
Saint Paul, Minnesota 55114-1065

(323) 857-1115/http://www.greeninteger.com

First English language edition 2003
English Translation©2003 Anni Whissen
©1960 by the Estate of Ole Sarvig
Published by agreement with the Leonhardt & HøierAgency aps.
Published originally as *Havet under mit vindue*
(Copenhagen: Gyldendal, 1960)

Design: Per Bregne
Typography: Guy Bennett
Photograph: Photograph of Ole Sarvig, ©Jesper Dijohn Pressefoto

LIBRARY OF CONGRESS CATALOGING IN PUBLICATION DATA
Sarvig, Ole
The Sea Below My Window
ISBN: 1-892295-79-2
p. cm — Green Integer 72
I. Title II. Series III. Translators

Green Integer books are published for Douglas Messerli
Printed in the United States of America on acid-free paper.

CHAPTER ONE · *The Window*

A voice, a distant voice, is calling: "Michael, Michael!"—but the call is drowned, and there's only the roar of the sea. Or is it my blood?...

The first thing I notice in the dim light that surrounds me on all sides is the shimmering, almost pulsating cracks of light that invade the room and hurt my eyes.

That this is a room all right is something my senses must have assured themselves of automatically even before I'm completely awake. I gain consciousness now, gradually, as if my consciousness were a liquid and my heartbeats slowly pumping consciousness into that something that's me. I hear the bed creaking under me and become aware of the damp, musty odor of the sheets, which have another strange smell as well. Then I begin to make out the white, plastered walls and the naked, unlit light bulb hanging from the middle of the ceiling. As I wake up to a never-ending bewilderment that hasn't yet turned to fear, and as the room's simple furnishings begin to invade my space through the little hollow at the corner of my eye, the sound that woke me up approaches. It towers outside of the room I can see, rising and thundering so that the cracks of light suddenly flash black. With a scream that surprises me because I don't recognize this shrill voice, I cover my ears with my hands while spinning around and burying my face in the pillow, which is damp and heavy and salty with the faint smell of soap or perfume.

I observe these minute details and go over them in my mind during these moments, as I lie there with my eyes closed and without breathing. I know this because deep down in my consciousness I think they're keeping that other something away, because that other something is about to come closer. Finally I can't hold it back any longer. I have to breathe again and hear the sound again, which is still as loud as it ever was. I must make an effort to sit up in bed and turn my glance toward the closed wooden shutters, which are letting in rays of light and sending waves of heat in my direction, and behind which that terrible thundering roar is located, loud and persistent. It is then that I hear my own voice for the second time, a voice that continues to be unfamiliar and that sounds as if a long silence were being shattered. I feel my lips moving quite mechanically, forming the words with the cushions of my lips and with that dry little muscle I have inside my mouth.

"My God," I say. "Where am I?"

Later on it's as if I forget that threatening sound. Anesthetized by it and as if in a trance, I sit up in bed, and now it's my hands that begin to act mechanically. They find their way down over my hips, which are narrow like a boy's. One hand touches the pubic hairs of my pelvic area and then grabs hold as if it were looking for something, while the other comes to rest on my knee. Then the other hand moves on, up under my short, unfamiliar nightgown, grabbing hold of my small breasts, which barely fill my hand, one after the other. Eventually I look down and notice that my skin is tanned and that there's a line on it as if from a bathing suit. Then everything turns black for a moment while I still sit slumped over in the bed. Did I pass out? I don't know.

The next thing I remember is that fear has taken hold of me. I've become conscious of it, and my hands are already behind my neck as if to protect it. They brush my short, soft hair and then hurry on as if they had touched fire. But later they press against my temples so it hurts, because I'm about to scream again. Only the scream doesn't come, and much later I finally feel my trembling, sweaty fingers venturing across my face, to my forehead and my eyes and my nose, touching my cheeks and my mouth and my chin, all of which are intact, smooth and unscarred.

I stare for the longest time at my hands, which are slender and tanned with unpainted, oval nails that mechanically dig into my palms before my very eyes.

My eyes are wide open now, and it's as if they constantly grow larger in this dim light. I sit there anesthetized by the thundering sound, no longer hearing it, sit there with wide open eyes like a little animal and feel my teeth, which are small and sharp and a bit crooked. But when I remove my hand from my mouth and notice I've bitten my knuckle so that it bleeds, I can't hold back my tears any longer. They well up from another darkness that I can't see. They wash over me and give me peace as I lie there slumped on the bed, keeping my hand away so that the blood doesn't drip on the sheet but on the pillow instead. At last only my sobs remain, louder than any other sound. My mouth becomes salty and wet, and I can't get the words out.

"Who am I?" I sob, my mouth full of salt. "Who could I possibly be, and where am I?"

When I notice the mirror over on the wall, I carefully prop myself up on my elbow and soundlessly put my feet on the cool, smooth floor tiles. I gingerly take a couple of steps over there as if I were afraid someone might keep me from my venture, prevent me from looking at that pale, fair face with its cropped features and those dark blue eyes. A moment later they peer out at me from the dark glass, cunning and terrified, as if, with my three steps across the floor in my bare feet, I had tried to fool the powers of life or death.

But I can't stand looking in the mirror, for the face I see is unfamiliar. I turn away in embarrassment, as if I had seen something I wasn't supposed to see. My glance continues to wander toward the low, unpainted table and the high-backed chair where a pile of clothes is lying that are unfamiliar, too, but that look as if they might belong to a woman my age.

It is then that I finally go over to the closed, shuttered window, but when I grope for the latch to the shutters, a strange scream slips out of me again. The wood is scorching hot, and my hands retreat. The roar behind the hot wood is even louder as my hands move forward again. I feel as if my blood is roaring, and I'm afraid of passing out once more. Finally I locate the latch. It is hot like the handle on a kettle, but I get it unlatched so that not just the wooden shutters, hot, dry, and rough, but both sides of the window as well swing out on their hinges and disappear from view to either side of the window opening.

I don't know what I've been expecting to see. I have a feeling that I stand there for a long time without understanding why. I see nothing, absolutely nothing through the window from where I'm standing with smarting eyes, inside the room behind the table. I close my eyes, protecting them with my hands, but not until there's an enormous gust of wind and I feel the cool air on my burning face does the roaring sound find its way into my consciousness as if I had been deaf for a moment in the bright light. Then I push the table aside, and when I lean out into the blue nothingness outside the window, I see the ocean foaming deep down below, breaking way down there against the rock that the house is perched on.

Slowly my eyes try to locate the horizon. Just below the window the water is protected, almost still. I notice seaweed and rocks and schools of little fishes in the green water, which is crisscrossed by moving shadows and has patches of quivering, needle-like rays on the surface. The sun is low, and the needles hurt my eyes, which must have been in the dim light for a long time. I wonder just how long?

"It's afternoon," I think, as I stand by the window on this spot in the world that I've no idea where is. I squint and stare out into the light, and where the flashes of sunlight and the billowing white crests of the waves formed by the squalls recede in the distance, I begin to see a long, low, hazy tongue of land with a lighthouse on it.

There are no boats or ships around, and the only living things I notice are the fish. As I lean out again, I can see all the way to the right the edge of the rock that the house is perched on. A few small white houses without windows are perched on top of it, and at the end of a courtyard or an alley, I see a low, whitewashed wall. There's still not a living soul around. I push the table again, since it's in the way, and when I kneel on the chair over there by the other windowsill, which is scorching hot from the sun, I notice that the rock continues around a little bay and that there's a beach below it.

A dark figure is walking down there, picking up something. As I lean out and happen to push the window so that it swings on its hinge and a flash arcs across the bay, the figure quickly turns its face in my direction only to turn away again as it continues its search on the beach. It's a man, and he looks like a fisherman as he walks hunched over at the edge of the shadow cast by the high, yellow slopes beyond.

He no longer looks in my direction, and my eyes slowly let go of him, only to discover that on top of the cliff there's a church-like building in a style that I don't recognize and a garden or a courtyard with green trees. Here two other persons are walking back and forth very slowly until they finally emerge at the edge of the cliff and stand for a while staring over toward my window. Then they disappear in the shrubbery, and I can no longer see them.

I lean out even farther, looking along the side of the house. It's a large house, whitewashed, with a lot of windows above and below me and along both sides. My window is in the middle of the house, and it appears to be the only one that's open. Farther down there's a balcony, which apparently hasn't been used for a long time. Chicken wire has been stretched between the sturdy cement balusters, which are peeling, and for a moment I wonder what purpose the chicken wire is supposed to serve. Then I notice the rats scampering along the narrow uppermost edge of the cliff and scurrying in and out of some pipes that look like drains from the house. I shiver involuntarily, but even so I follow one of them with my eyes toward a low, empty terrace, which is slimy and green with algae and has steps leading down to the sea. There are three or four rats over there, and they seem to be eating some small fishes or some bait that has been left behind by someone who has been sitting there fishing.

I look over toward the beach again. The fisherman is gone, but when I direct my glance up toward the cliff, I just happen to see his back disappearing through an opening in the white wall above. It looks as if there are some low roofs behind the wall. Maybe a street? Maybe the beginning of a town extending down over the hill on the other side where I can't see it?

A little further along the wall of the house close to the window I'm leaning out of, I suddenly discover two narrow boarded-up windows. I haven't noticed those before, but now I stare at them as if I'm expecting them to provide the answer to my riddle.

"I wonder who lives there?" my dry lips and the long unused muscle of my tongue mumble mechanically. I think in a flash, so that the two thoughts become one, that it's English I'm speaking and that maybe those are windows belonging to the very room I myself have access to. I try hard, try to remember, but my memory disappears like the spine of a fish that's heading for the deep: I remember absolutely nothing. As far as I can tell, I've never been in this place before.

"This place...this place!?" I mumble, and I don't know what I mean by that, but once more I feel this inexplicable fear rising in me that makes me shiver even though the sun is shining and both the sill and the table are burning hot.

I slip down off the chair and stand with my naked feet on the tile floor in my unfamiliar nightgown. Bewildered I look once more at my hands as if they don't belong to me, and I see that my nails are starting to dig into my palms again, where deep red marks remain from before.

I feel that the scream is getting closer again, but I mustn't scream, I think to myself, I must do something: I'll get dressed! But when I stand there naked on the floor with my arms raised above my head, I notice a deep scar on the inside of my right arm as if it had been broken and operated on. I collapse and just make it to the bed. And now I lie there again, lie there for a long time with dry eyes and a nauseating feeling that gradually fills my entire body as I touch and squeeze my scarred arm, which is paler and a bit thinner than the other one.

Shivering with cold, I finally get up and begin to put on the clothes that are lying on the chair. There's a yellow linen skirt and a blue blouse, and it occurs to me that women my age wear clothes like these all over the world. But I don't know where that thought comes from or what I mean by "all over the world," for I know nothing about myself. Nothing at all. Only that the scar on my arm already has become strangely familiar, as if this trace of pain alone vaguely connects me with what has been my life somewhere else and what is now beyond my reach. I also find underwear, sandals, and a pair of slacks—and a long, white wool cardigan that I put on because I'm cold.

I feel something in the pocket of the cardigan and pull it out. It's a new billfold of plain leather, and when I open it over by the table, green and brown and red and blue bills come tumbling out. They are printed in a language I can't read but which seems familiar after all. I pick up the bills one by one, examining them. On one of them there's a picture of an old-fashioned coach with footmen.

Have I ever seen a coach like that? On the other side there's a picture of a stern face below a white wig. A judge? How do I know that judges wear wigs? Is it in England that they do that? But this is not, cannot be England. I shiver again in my heavy cardigan and grab one of the other bills. On one side there is the face of a bearded man and on the other side statues between clipped trees and a white cross in the background. Or is it supposed to be a cemetery?

Involuntarily I tremble and push the bills back into the billfold, but I remain standing with it clasped in my hand. I notice to my amazement, as if from the distance, my fingers feeling it as if they were looking for something and opening it again. There's no metal in it, no coins or jewelry, but in one of the folds there's a note with a stamp on it and a not very clearly written name. It starts with an M-, and it looks as if it also ends in an -m. I try to spell my way through it and conclude that it says *Miriam.* Could that be my name? The stamp is indistinct just like the name, and I can't read the printed text. It's in the same language as the bills. Besides, I have the impression that the note is a receipt.

I put it down on the table because my hand is shaking as I try once more to make head or tail out of the printed words. I don't get far. The language is vaguely familiar, but I can't read it. I pull out the bills again and examine them. On one of the little green bills there's a picture of a large house with columns and portals. Is it possible that I've been in a house like that before and experienced something unpleasant there? Something that's related to this difficulty I'm having spelling my way through this foreign language and to this feeling that I ought to be able to understand the words on the bill, which I put away again now because a sinister face emerges on it in a round, white field, as I hold it up to the light.

I look around the room, which is mercilessly empty except for the bedding and the extra items of clothing on the chair. In the drawer of the nightstand I find a comb, a lipstick, and a cheap watch that would fit a fourteen-year-old boy. The watch has stopped. There's also an open pack of yellow cigarettes made from a dark tobacco and a box of matches. When I open it, I notice that a couple of the matches have been spent, and when I bend down later to buckle my sandal and happen to look under the bed, I discover four cigarette butts. That's exactly the number of cigarettes missing in the pack. So someone must have smoked them here, in this room. I pick up the butts and stand with them in my hand for a moment before throwing them out the window. There's a faint trace of lipstick—"my" lipstick—on one of them.

I walk over to the mirror, comb my hair, and put on lipstick, and I'm amazed at my dexterity: I must have painted my mouth thousands of times before. But where? And for whom? Once more I take a look at my small, fair, sunburned face. It is probably twenty-five years old with dark blue eyes, round chin, turned-up nose, and light hair cut very short like a boy's. I meet my own questioning eyes. My face is calm now, and there's a little determined pull around my mouth that I didn't notice before.

Then I walk over to the only door in the room, a double glass door with heavy drapes on the other side. I see myself as a blurry figure in the glass pane. I try the key and discover that the door isn't locked, and it suddenly occurs to me that maybe someone is waiting for me on the other side who will open the door in a minute or pull the drapes aside and stare at me. I feel weak, and I notice again this sickening feeling of fear rising in me. But I've already turned the handle. The door opens, and I step into another room.

It's empty. I stand there for the longest time listening and looking into the dim light. But the room is empty. It seems damp and cold like a basement, and at first I don't think there are any windows. But after my blinded eyes have grown accustomed to the darkness, I see a few faint cracks of light and walk over and open the shutters.

Outside there's a narrow alley with low, white-washed houses on the other side. There are no windows in the closest houses, only doors, and those are all closed. I keep staring out through the dirty panes but see only the peeling plaster of the houses and the indistinct, dark wood of the doors on the other side of the alley. I'm about to turn away from the window when I hear steps sounding down at the bottom of the alley and see the head and back moving past of a woman dressed in black. Behind her, at some distance, a man follows, likewise dressed in black and with a large, black, broad-brimmed hat.

I look around the room, which has a low, round table with three plain, low armchairs around it. There is also a couch and a stove, and, built into the wall behind a brown-painted door with wrought iron, I discover a closet, which turns out to be empty except for a pair of dirty shoes and a raincoat that looks as if it would fit me. I examine the pockets and find a brass-yellow key and two green tickets with torn-off corners. Needless to say, they're printed in the same language as the bills and the mysterious receipt. I'm just about to crumple them up and throw them away when I suddenly jump as I hear my own laughter resounding hollowly from the naked walls, which breathe dampness toward me like white sheets. I also know what it is that makes me laugh, because there's no doubt about the fact that "cine," whatever language it may be, means "cinema," and that the person who wore the coat last went to the movies and bought green tickets for some film or other and sat there next to a boyfriend or girlfriend, next to a man or a woman, in the 24th row number 7 or 8 in the local movie theater in this place, which I have no idea where is.

Just as little idea as I have about who I am and why this has happened. Everything goes black again. I have to sit down for a moment on one of the chairs in this empty room, which looks like a waiting room, and where the only sound is the roar of the sea below my window.

The next room is completely empty, just a hall-way. When I open the shutters out toward the al-ley on my way toward a door that's half ajar in the other corner, I suddenly hear steps outside the large, closed, brown-painted door with the solid lock right in front of me.

The steps are heavy. They must be those of a man. They slowly come up the stairs, walk past, while I hold my breath on my side of the door. The steps stop higher up. I strain my ears but hear nothing but the roar of the sea and my own heart hammering away as if it were about to burst.

No doors bang, no voices are heard, and there are no more steps. But a little while later the steps suddenly come down the stairs again, slowly, as if someone had stopped on a landing higher up, listening as I myself have been listening. The steps stop for a moment outside of where I stand, and it seems to me that I hear a hand scratching at the door. When the steps have disappeared down the stairs and out into the alley again, and I'm certain I can no longer hear them, I suddenly look down at my hands. The red marks in my palms have become deeper and redder, and one of them is bleeding.

I now walk through the other door, the one that's standing ajar, and open the shutters into what turns out to be a little bathroom and a kitchen facing the sea. They seem dusty and bare in the glaring light of the setting sun, and the roar of the surf down below is so strong now that the tips of my fingers tingle when I touch walls or tables or the pots that clatter on their hooks above the stove.

There's nothing in the bathroom except a toothbrush and cup, a towel, a piece of soap, and a jar of face cream, which has not yet been unwrapped from its yellow wrapping paper. I unwrap it and put some cream on my face and my burning hands.

Later I think about the fact that apparently I must be in the process of coming to terms with this strange and fantastic situation when I assume, just like that, that the things I see around me are mine or meant for me.

I stand in the kitchen and feel the floor vibrating through my soles from the surf way down below. A pile of dry wood is lying under the stove, which looks as if it hasn't been used for a long time. The empty drawers in the painted table squeak when I pull them out. The dusty knives and forks with broken tines, which rattle around in the drawer, don't seem to have been used for a long time either. But in a large green-painted meat-safe I find bread, cheese, butter, and smoked meat, all of it neatly wrapped in newspaper. There is also a bottle of wine.

I lose no time reaching for the wine bottle, because I'm dying of thirst. Before I drink, I hold it up to the light and see it shining like a red stone that I must have seen sometime or other; for I think of a clear, red stone as I sniff the bottle, hesitating, but finally drinking anyway. I break off an end of the bread and begin gnawing at the cheese; then I drink some of the dry red wine again. I stand with the bottle in my hand, looking at its pale green, printed label, which has only one word on it. "Vino" it says. Could I be in Italy? Or maybe in Portugal? Or in Spain? For a moment I'm also vaguely reminded of South or Central America or of Mexico. Where am I? And what do I actually know about these countries that I'm trying so hard to think of? It's as if my mouth is about to say something, but as it turns out, it's just a hoarse clearing of the throat. In a strange way I'm afraid of my own voice, but for a moment I somehow feel protected by the roar of the sea down below. I put the bottle to my lips again and drink greedily so that the wine trickles down my chin.

Later on I unfold the newspaper. The name of it is "LA ISLA." It's written in large print right across the front page, and it's the only thing I can read even though many words still seem familiar to me. Some of the pages are so faded that I can barely see the letters. There's only one picture in the paper. I guess it's supposed to be a person, but the newspaper is printed so poorly that I can't make out if it's a man or a woman. All I can see is a blurry, human-looking shape.

So maybe the name of the place—or the town—

is "La Isla"? It's got to be the same as the French "île," I think. *The island!* I mumble to myself. It can't mean anything else. I guess I must be on an island...

But *where*? And *who*? Something hammers away in my brain and my blood as I stare at the black front page of the newspaper again, until I suddenly discover way up at the top a name written in pencil.

"Sra. de Maritza" it says. Who was it that used to call me "signorina"? For that's got to be what the word means—or at least something like that. Maybe my name is Maritza, and maybe it says Maritza on the other note. I take it out again to compare, but it's too hard to read. It could just as well be one as the other. Still it seems to me that it's another name that's on it, more like Miriam. Could they have made a mistake? Or am I Maritza's signorina and Maritza the maid who has bought me all these things?—Or...I suddenly start, gripped by a terrifying suspicion, for I hear far away this word "signorina." "Signorina," a hissing voice shouts at me, and I perceive a figure coming closer and taking my light away and bending over me…

With trembling hands I put the newspaper back in the empty cupboard with the food. Then I unlock the door to the stairs with the key I found in the raincoat. Only after I've locked the door behind me again does it occur to me that I never doubted for a moment that the key would fit. I must have used it before!

My sandals clip-clop down the tiles of the staircase, and the raincoat, which I'm carrying over my arm, brushes against the bare, plastered walls. I step out into the empty alley and begin walking in the same direction that the woman and the man dressed in black disappeared in just a little while ago.

CHAPTER TWO · *The Little Town*

The sun doesn't reach the alley, and it's already getting dark. I can hear the sea behind the walls, and I don't know why I can't shake this feeling that all the white I see around me on the house walls is just a shell of plaster, just like a thin layer of ashes, thin like an eggshell, and that it'll make the same sound as an eggshell when it bursts. But I don't have the nerve to reach out for it. I make a fist in the pocket of my cardigan to keep my hand from trembling. I press it toward me so that it hurts as I walk on through the deserted, strangely angular alley, behind which the sea roars.

There are whitewashed stairs and narrow, white alleys everywhere, and driven by an instinct that I now suspect may have become a habit, I rush down a couple of stairs, turn a corner, and come out into a wider street below.

It's wide enough for a car to get through here, but I see no cars, only two deep tracks from a narrow vehicle on the rough, brown clay that fills the street, which has spots and puddles after a rain. The street is fairly long, lying there with its white walls and closed shutters and with a strange oppressive heat wafting from the houses.

They disappear in a soft curve in both directions, and I slowly, hesitantly, begin walking toward a red glow of light that flickers on the ash-white walls, making them look almost violet in the dusk. Here the sea is only a distant roar behind the walls, and it's completely still in the street except for a low, crackling sound that seems to come from the flickering glow.

Fear paralyzes my senses, and I feel rather than see that not all the shutters are closed. In fact, they are open toward the interior, and dark figures, whose faces I can't make out, sit and stand in the dark, inside the open doors and gates. I startle when a frail, dark silhouette, which could only be that of a child, darts across the street from one dark doorway to another on the opposite side.

I have tried to stifle a cry, and it's as if this sound brings the faces out in the doorways now, at first pale and indistinct, but a little later quite bright from the fires flickering across their foreheads and eyes, once I reach the more densely populated part of the street where the fire basins blaze outside the doors. A faint murmur of voices can be heard from inside of the houses. Here and there old women in long, dark skirts sit on their haunches blowing into the fire or poking it with a stick, while the men— dark-skinned, dark-eyed, and dark-haired—stand in the doorways with the fires flickering across their faces and stare after me as I walk past.

I enter a little square where the street has widened around a well. From there several broad, pebbled steps lead upward between the shuttered houses, some of which have spindly balconies with large plants on them, making the place look like a cemetery. Three women in shawls and long, black skirts are filling their jars at the well. Across from them, up against the white, peeling wall, which looks like a snowscape viewed from high above (What could I possibly know about snowscapes?), two little girls are standing on tiptoe stretching to lay a bouquet of flowers on the shelf under a picture of the Virgin. A naked light bulb illuminates the Virgin's head. Below the picture, in a kind of wheelchair, sits a fat woman dressed in black. She has no legs. At this point the deep, narrow tracks that I saw way down the street disappear. No one looks at me. No one seems to notice me. I feel for a moment as if I have no body and can walk right through these other figures, and they through me. Fear has taken hold of me again, and I don't dare to stop. I walk on, as if I know deep down that there's something I have to do. I hurry forward till I almost run while casting a glance in the direction of the woman in the wheelchair. Her long, iron-gray hair has come undone under the black shawl, which has now slipped down around the back of the seat of the chair so that her enormous, white, naked arms shine in the dusk.

As I walk on, I see more steps and streets leading upward. I can make out a large, gray, somewhat sloping wall, like that of a fortress or castle high up, and behind it the outlines of other houses and rooftops. Now the street widens and becomes a quiet square with large, fluted trees around a roughhewn stone church whose doors stand open. Inside the doors is darkness. I notice a single candle flickering in the dark as I walk by and slip into an alley behind the trees. A moment later I'm standing by the harbor.

I stop in amazement and look around. I don't know this place any more than I know the fire-flickering streets and dark squares I've just walked through. But I'm not really sure either that I've never seen these places before, albeit possibly just one single time, but if so under completely different circumstances which I remember nothing, absolutely nothing about.

In any case, everything that I see now is new and strange to me: the low hills on the horizon with houses that are white as seashells; the bay in front of the calm, shimmering water; the pier that I'm standing on and along which two old-fashioned sailboats lie moored in the still waters next to some shell-shaped, dark blue fishing boats. Farther out toward the jetty is a coal-black steamer whose puffing, sooty smoke is in strange contrast to the still water. As it rises into the air, the column of smoke is flattened by the wind and forced out over the bay in a thin fan.

A dusty, wide street lined with an irregular row of low, white houses runs along the pier. Where these recede, there are open squares in several places with trees and chairs and tables in front of cafés and pavilions. The promenade along the harbor seems to be part of a deserted tourist resort. Except that over by the fourth pavilion across from the smoking steamer a couple has sat down, and at another table there's a single figure. It's a woman. I see her turning her head and craning her neck as if she were looking around for someone. For the longest time I look in her direction, but it's not me she's looking for.

I walk over to the nearest pavilion with tables and empty chairs in front and sit down. I'm still afraid of my own voice and say nothing when a young, dark boy in a white waiter's jacket comes out to take my order; I simply point to the steaming espresso machine inside on the counter by the bar. He nods impassively and disappears. Maybe it's my imagination, but I have the impression he is deliberately avoiding my gaze.

I drink the coffee, which does me a world of good. I even get up enough nerve to order a second cup by calling the boy. He answers "Yes, Madam" in poor English and then adds a couple of words in his own language that I don't understand.

Over by the next pavilion, which is completely empty, a shoeshine boy has emerged. He sits on his brass-mounted box, picking his teeth and looking out over the water. Why doesn't he come over here? I think, at the same time looking down at my feet and finding the answer: My white sandals are not exactly the kind you shine. Shoeshine boys know their prey.

Over on the sailboats the sailors are working slowly and steadily with their rolls and bundles of roping. The black smoke is still puffing silently out of the chimneys on the black steamer. The woman way over there is sitting still now and staring out over the water. Every few minutes, though, she continues to look around in all directions as if she were looking for someone. Out on the low hills, which are just receiving the last, faint, rose-colored glow from the setting sun, I now notice ten to twenty old-fashioned windmills turning with wreaths of shining, light-colored sails. They look like giant, faded dandelions that the wind is doing its best to strip bare out there in the hills. It's completely protected where I'm sitting, but high above me thin, jagged clouds rush by. I can hear the roar of the sea very faintly on the other side of town, and I get cold shivers again when I think about the apartment on the sea where I woke up a few hours ago and which I left to wander out into this nearly deserted town. It is getting darker and darker with only the glow of the fires flickering from the back alleys, as if the houses were ovens, and now flickering across a verdigrised monument as well over there where I haven't been yet. The monument consists of figures on the look-out, men and women, entire family groups. For just one moment I think they're alive, that it's the families of the town standing over there looking out over the water; but they are merely statues, standing immobile in stone or metal, arrested on their way toward a corner of the world they'll never reach and unable to return to the large, clumsy, and strangely foreign building behind them, which is built in the same style as the monument and which looks like a large desk set.

As darkness falls and the windmills recede in the distance, a high pealing sound enters my consciousness just like the first hint of pain when a migraine is coming on. (Now, how would I happen to know that?) Out of the street with the flickering fires behind the clumsy building that looks like a desk set, a throng of white shirts moves past nimbly and low above dozens of thin, black, tripping legs silhouetted against the fires. In the middle of this procession of white-shirted, dark-skinned boys, that I can barely make out and that seems dream-like and unreal as it glides forward toward the water, walks an older boy. In his hands, which are raised high, he rings what appears to be a silver bell. When he stops for a moment, the pealing sound comes to a stop, too. Behind him, under a canopy walks a very pale, older, heavy-set priest in vestments that seem redder than the fire. He holds a gleaming, golden object against his forehead, and I understand, without knowing how I know, that he must be the bishop. I have raised myself halfway up in my seat in my eagerness to see the rear of the procession. It is brought up by a tall, young priest with a slight limp, who is dressed in black vestments and who has a large, frizzy head of hair. I follow them closely with my eyes as if my own fate depended on the pealing bell down there by the water. The procession stops, and I notice that a coffin, which has been brought out of the darkness, is now being lowered into the hull of a ship after a short ceremony. I keep staring while gripping the arm of the chair so hard that my hands hurt and my knuckles turn white. It is not until now that I notice a young fellow with flaxen hair and blue eyes, which look pale even here in the dusk, standing outside the café's most distant tables staring at me. He doesn't resemble anyone else I've seen in this town. He's dressed as if he has come from work on one of the ships, but his dark work shirt accentuates his slight build and his narrow shoulders. As his gaze meets mine and he turns away and begins to walk over toward the houses, I notice they slope considerably.

At this moment the lights suddenly come on everywhere. The monument is surrounded by four large, violet globes that give the illusion of being freely suspended in the air in the same way that the long, spread-out row of identical lamps illuminating the whole pier and continuing out onto a distant jetty doesn't seem to be attached anywhere either.

All of a sudden the lights dim, leaving behind a row of yellow-green jellyfish where the globes were, but it lasts only a few seconds, then the violet globes are back on again, and all the houses show a yellowish light behind the empty crosses of the windows or behind the silhouettes of men and women, standing immobile in the window openings, as if they already had been standing around watching for a long time what took place on the pier.

I look around me. The procession has quickly disappeared as if it had fled a lurking wave coming from the dark, glistening water.

Now there's more life, with more people on the promenade, or maybe I just didn't notice them before. A few have settled down at the café tables down the line, but I'm still alone in front of my kiosk. My glance searches for the woman out there by the bar at the far end. For the longest time I am unable to locate her, but then I discover she's no longer alone. A slender young fellow is with her, and he's just getting up. He takes his leave and begins walking in my direction, and I think for a moment that he'll pass by me quite close, just as close as the young sailor with the flaxen hair a moment ago. But he turns off. It's as if he has seen me, because for a moment he looks right at me but then quickly turns his face away, as if not to meet my gaze, and walks over toward the fire-flickering alleys. I see him push back a long, unruly forelock, and this movement instantly brings back to me his narrow, pointed face with the heavy brows and the sad, dark blue eyes with black markings, even though his back disappears in the alley at this point, leaving me behind paralyzed with my empty glass and between empty chairs. I know this man! And he knows me—and is avoiding me. But who is he ? And why is he avoiding me? I bite my lip, for I feel tears and powerlessness and fear crowding in, but I mustn't scream, mustn't break down here in this place, where hundreds of eyes are watching me from the houses behind my back.

I look around for the woman, but she, too, has disappeared by now. The pier is almost empty. Two groups of very young girls with pale complexions and dark hair and simple, bright-colored dresses keep strolling past the pavilions arm in arm. Then I hear this strange panting close by and quickly turn around. It's a thin, gypsy-like woman dressed in unbelievable tatters who is walking two large, black German shepherds right past my table. The dogs want to sniff me. Their pink tongues hang out of their throats, and I feel their breath. One of them begins to growl, and the woman yanks them away from me. She talks aloud to herself as she walks on, swaying in her flat shoes and leaning back because of the pull of the dogs.

I am paralyzed, paralyzed with fear of this riddle standing around me in stone and dust and flesh and fire. This fire that only the water and its infinity can extinguish. These images and this presence, which only the enormous, curved, blind eye of the sea can forget. I think of the sea; I know the sea… Maybe I carry it within me, I think, but I've also *seen* it, in fact, have just now seen it.

I've come out into a long street full of blind walls and large gates. In the light issuing forth, now white and now red, from an old smithy, some boys are playing outside an open gate. They are wearing short boots and caps and odd-looking, long jackets. They look like the sort of boys you see in old engravings (What engravings?) or in photographs that I must have seen sometime in the past. An absolutely fantastic thought takes hold of me, and fear ensnares my throat with a fine cord. Deep

40

down inside me, I hear a shrill, distant laughter, and I stop, barely daring to breathe. Behind me the boys go on playing without paying any attention to me, and in front of me on both sides of the street I see long rows of cabs and old-fashioned, tall, gray-painted buses with white roofs, blue glass shades in front of the windshields, and worn brass handles hanging below radiators with a dull shine. Farther down the street, I seem to see even older models and large, square lanterns belonging to horse-drawn carriages. The thought is mad, but I feel as if I'm on my way back into the past and as if the air I'm leaning against at this moment is a pane that won't permit me to take one more step forward but wants to force me back past the smithy and the playing boys, in the direction of the hotel's glass door that I just came out of.

I know I won't walk through that door again. The dark figure has made it through the hall and is standing behind the glass at the end of the street watching me. Maybe it's my imagination, but I see the door opening, catching the flickering glow now white from the forge, because when I look in that direction again a few seconds later, it is closed, and there's no one in the street except the playing boys and the long, silent row of vehicles from a distant past.

But in my panic I'm already on my way into an alley leading through gardens and hedges over toward a row of tall houses with lights in the windows. Along the path there's a ditch with glistening, running water. Farther along, the ditch widens into a little pond where ducks are swimming and where a single swan shines phosphorous-white in the dark. At the same time, the path runs right by a ramshackle shed nailed together from scraps of board on whose sides and ledges there are all sorts of plants, dripping as if they had just been watered. The drops glisten in the glow from the little oil lamp that hangs smoking between the plants, and I now see a fat woman with a thick pigtail down her back standing there with a watering can in her hands. She smiles as I walk past, putting down her watering can and handing me a large, wax-like flower which she has picked from a dainty bush by the shed. She also says something in that language I can't understand and smilingly shakes her head when I offer a few words of thanks in my own language.

Encouraged I continue walking, getting in between the houses, walking through empty streets that are virtually in darkness. Again I hear the high sound of the silver bell and see the throng of boys in white shirts whirling past at the end of the street. The small of my back reminds me that the streets are rising, and I notice they are getting steeper and steeper. Suddenly I step from a dark cross alley out into a little square with a dark stone pavilion with stacks of boxes and sacks between the columns. A closed-up market. In front of me there's a high ramp paved with smooth, round stones, and at the end of the ramp there's a gate.

I walk up through the gate which is flanked by pale stone figures without heads and arms but in classical garb. Here I get into another part of the city, at first through a courtyard with porticos and black bronze lions worn smooth by numerous hands, then through steep, winding, poorly lighted streets with smooth paving stones between white walls up and up again until I'm suddenly standing in the shadow of an enormous building that seems tall and dark like a mountain after the last low, plastered houses.

There are towers and spires way up there. And still it's as if I sense rather than actually see that it's the cathedral. Maybe it's the faint, almost inaudible singing coming from the rock that tells me this. It sounds like the sea far away and deep down or like your own rushing blood when you hold one of the large porcelain-heavy conches up to your ear. (I wonder when I ever did that?) Everything is dark here around the cathedral, the street lights must have gone out. Only high up the rough face of granite, a colored glow of light forces its way out, but I'm too close to be able to see the stained glass windows that must be there.

I feel my way along with my hand, holding on to the cold, damp stone (which reminds me of a place I've been at one time, only where?) as I walk around the rock of the cathedral. The distant song comes closer but stops the moment my hand, which is following the rock, grips the dark, empty air. I'm standing in a portal, and when I slowly come closer, in toward the glow of light, I hear the high, clear voice of a man: "In nomine patris, et filii, et spiritus sancti …"

Those are the first words I've understood in this place. This is the beginning. In front of me I see a beautiful scene in the distance. Framed by the vaulted door opening facing the long aisle of the cathedral, there's a small group of people far away: a man and a woman with a child in a long, white gown that a priest is in the process of baptizing. Three times he pours water from the baptismal font over the child's head. Shadows busy themselves around the group and bring the priest some metal object that glistens as it catches the light; and the child has already started crying in there in that distant scene, filling the invisible vaulting of the cathedral with its sobs, when I turn away, as the dark backs bend deeper over the child. The last thing I see is a glimpse of a silvery, lighted altar in a chapel far away. It's like the daylight at the end of the long tunnel.

I keep seeing these scenes before me as I leave the cathedral and enter a street that slopes slightly downward and looks as if it's lighted farther down. It's as if I've had a look into another age, I think, a distant past with close and familiar figures that can be found hidden from my own vision in a ray of sunshine in the darkness of my mind; and another age, a more recent and puzzling time of blinding light at the end of the long tunnel of my vision.

Am I on my way toward that light? Are we always on our way toward the light like a shining, blinding opening out of time and darkness? I ask myself as I walk on. I don't know where these words come from, because I'm not aware that I've ever had such thoughts before or that I've inherited such words. Is that what it's all about? Always under way? Always alone? Under way from this other group in the half darkness, from these beings who will always follow us, never completely pale around us, no matter where we are, but who can be found around us in those closest to us, in those we meet, even if we travel across the sea…

The sea. Suddenly it gets dark before my eyes, and my thoughts and senses vanish. I'm standing in a paved, slightly sloping street between low houses. The street has widened into a small square here, and in front of me there's a fountain in the middle of which the water trickles out through the sloping lips of four well-worn metal faces. Several of the houses have open folding doors into the kitchens, where women in long skirts are stirring steaming pots, while the fire flickers out through the slits and holes in the stoves. The men are sitting together, two or more, on the stone steps in front of the houses, and in almost all the windows, which are open to let in the cool night air, are the little ones: boys and girls, waiting for food and sleep, silent in the dim light and with dark eyes in their faces, now pale and still, which are all turned in the direction of the square and the fountain, as if they were looking out the windows of a stopped train.

My steps resound as I walk on after having had a sip from one of the four jets of water. I feel the children's blurry faces turning to look after me in the silence and following me into a new sloping street with new thousands of dark, curved, dully glistening paving stones that my shoes slip on so that I have to hold on to the walls of the houses.

Now the street disappears, still sloping, in through a gate that continues into a pale, lighted tunnel with prison-like iron grilles at the sides from where there's a draft of icy air. Sometimes there's also a whiff of flowers as if there might be gardens somewhere down there in the darkness.

It's the city gate I've walked through. In front of me is the sea again, the low hills, and just one of the now otherwise invisible windmills silhouetted against the moon. The moon is larger than I ever recall having seen it (wherever that may have been?), and it's about to rise on the horizon. It looks like a sun-lit hill far away in a distant land, and it casts its light on this maze of paved paths and steps between gardens and houses, leading from the platform where I'm standing down to the plain and the outskirts of the lower part of town and possibly to that road which draws its long, phosphorescent streak up toward the horizon.

I begin the descent but lose my way in a garden. It stretches out downward and upward over countless terraces, and I've already walked down some, I no longer know how many. Around me are plants and trees, varieties that I don't recognize, reaching forward and upward like the images of the mind and of longing, rising with branch upon branch pointing toward this globe which has disappeared from space for a few hours and left behind the stained, uremic reflection of the moon, which is now letting go of the horizon out there; standing there, these plants themselves are a reflection, reminders of music I must have heard, of thoughts I must have had at some time (this memory that I don't have and yet have and of which I have kept only shadows and outlines!) A small tree close by stands there with the fragrance of its giant flowers, whose shapes are like bassoons in an orchestra that must have shaken my nerves at one time; and with a mass at its foot, a foam of varieties large as coins and small as moths, whose colors shine palely toward me in the moonlight: Women! I think, looking down at myself, down at my blouse and my skirt. Myriads of women as I myself am a woman, I think, and my hands secretly rush down over my body but then hastily flutter up to my mouth again so that my knuckle hurts, for someone is stirring in the garden close to me.

I see a shadow moving behind a bush, and over there in the other walk a larger one. For a long time I stand stiff and still until I suddenly start to laugh. For it's just a cat and a dog, a large, light-colored, shaggy dog that doesn't bark and means no harm, but just rubs itself against me and trots along.

Suddenly I'm a happy, little girl again as I scratch the bites from the flea it left behind. I stand there without fear, conscious of the silent, diamond-shaped flight of the bats around me; stand there, watching a swarm of ants in the moonbeam at my foot, far away like the traffic on a distant road that I've forgotten as well. I suddenly have all the time in the world. I've been walking for hours, and I can keep on walking for hours. The world is good, the dogs friendly, the bats exciting and soft like soot. The cats stir around me, and the ants make a wide arc around my foot, distant like the lanterns on the vehicles way out there on the road. It doesn't matter when I find my way out of the garden. As soon as I'm outside and back in town, something will be waiting for me, something that I simply have to do and that cannot wait: I must find out *everything*. But until then…

I don't know how long it takes me, but when I finally find a gate—after having wandered endlessly up and down terraces and through the garden paths, which form a mysterious pattern that I carry invisibly inside me now, just as I'm storing my hidden childhood—I have one major happy concern: I'm starved! I walk as I must have walked at one time as a child—out a gate, down a path. I have no particular place to go just as I didn't then. But I smile anyway, because in my hand I'm squeezing my billfold full of money. A childish confidence that almost makes me laugh out loud tells me in a little, worldly-wise voice that I won't be hungry for long, so I walk on, light-footed and carefree, with my mouth full of saliva to still that disquiet that is growing in my body now, which is hungry like that of a child's and not that much bigger.

I turn a sharp corner and am about to walk down the steps leading in between the houses I saw before from above, when I discover a strange cave with lights in the windows. There are tables in front, and the walls are covered with pebbles and shells from the beach, spelling out the word "café" in the middle of the wall.

I enter. There are no other guests. It's my destiny to be alone tonight. Behind a counter that opens up toward a little kitchen stands a gray-haired man preparing a meal. A younger woman with old-fashioned, medium-length yellowish hair with deep waves in it is sitting on a chair behind the counter reading. It could be his daughter, his wife, or maybe his mistress. I can't tell. She has tired, gray skin and tired, dark-brown eyes, which she directs at me now while mumbling what sounds like "bonsoir."

The man, too, says "bonsoir," while working away at the stove without turning his eyes away from what he's doing.

"Bonsoir," I say, sitting down at one of the red tables. "Could I please have something to eat?" I ask in the same breath in English. They nod, and I hear a faint "bien sûr." I look around while I wait. The walls are thickly covered with light-colored pebbles and shells. There are benches and tables along the walls, and at each table there's a large, serrated conch with an electric bulb in it made into a wall lamp. An artistic chandelier made out of crab shells hangs in the center of the room, and there are fishnets suspended from the ceiling and funny-looking dolls made out of roping in the corners.

There's also a bottle in the window that looks like a fat man, a "dinner guest" in top hat and tails. I smile to myself, wondering just where I have seen a character like that before, but I'm suddenly frightened when I notice a man standing outside on the path threatening me through the window. Then I begin to smile again, and I feel my smile getting broader while my eyes remain motionless, transfixed at the figure out there: it's a drunk having a long conversation with the empty chairs and tables. He disappears after a few minutes but returns again, threatening them.

The cook has noticed him. "Janine," he calls, and the woman gets up and walks over and bolts the door. "Un fou," she says, shrugging her shoulders.

The food is great: a spicy dish that I don't recall having had before. I eat in silence at my table, but the two take their meal in the kitchen. I try hard to recall the shape of the wineglass, the pottery with its miniature pattern, the pattern of the tablecloth, the walls, the shells, the dolls, the place, the two of them.

I can't. I haven't been here before. Their silent acceptance of my presence and the surly reception

I received are not meant for a customer who is familiar to them but rather for a new patron, whose language they don't speak. A new customer in a place that apparently is suffering from a lack of business.

I pay and notice that the money I have in my billfold is much more than sufficient. When I have paid, the woman, whose name is Janine, as I now know, lingers at my table. She picks up the flower I received from the fat, smiling woman down by the canals. I had carried it with me all the way and put it on the table.

"Passiflore!" she says, taking it over to the bar to show the man. They hold it up to the light, admiring it, and carefully put it back on my table. It's not until now that I take a look at it and discover that its anthers and styles are like a group of standing or kneeling persons with three figures raised high above the rest.

"Passiflore?" I repeat, mimicking the pronunciation, and the woman nods.

"Oui, très belle. Passiflore. Fleur de la passion."

I feel both her glance and that of the cook's resting on me for a long time, and to avoid their eyes I look down at the red table, from which the table-cloth has now been removed. I'm confused at this point, have almost stepped across an invisible threshold—because of that flower. I try telling myself that it doesn't mean anything. But I can't. I don't find it meaningless. The garden where I just felt an inexplicable happiness is far away now. It's as if I have stood on this spot many years ago, awake and alone among slumbering plants and stirring animals. Fear slowly returns, rising like a tide, imperceptible and icy with each wave, rising a little higher than the previous one and lapping at my happiness and childish contentment. I hardly notice that the woman, Janine, brings me a glass of wine, apparently as a gesture of friendship.

I slip into my own world, and it's as if my eyes get lost in the night, which I can see out there through the window. I seem to see the little throng of choirboys in their white shirts, whirling past in the moonlight over on the path, as if they were looking for something or someone. When they have disappeared from view between the low shrubs, I see clearly out there on the horizon a steamer whose chimney is smoking like an extinguished torch. It's all black in the moonlight. No lights can be seen on it, and it doesn't seem to move. Only after several minutes have gone by do I notice that it has moved in relation to the window frame and that it is coming this way. I close my eyes until it has completely disappeared from view while I think of the coffin that was brought on board the sailboat and of the other black steamer that lay smoking down by the harbor. I try to forget the two ships, but the thought of them keeps haunting me like a dream. A dream within the dream. That is me here. Me? I open my eyes and stare at the empty sea, but when I close them again, I see before me hundreds of enormous waves with nettle-like crests silently marching toward me, as if they were beings looking for me to stumble over. I bite my lip to keep from screaming and hurting my palms again with my nails and am grateful for the pain, for I will not…will not think that thought…

I'm alive. Something inexplicable has happened to me that I must find out about, and I have no time to spare. I get up, leaving the large wax flower on the table. Without a word I struggle with the door and get it unlatched. As I turn the next corner of the paved path, I see Janine standing in the doorway looking after me with her tired eyes, which now shine red in the light from the cave. At the same time I hear music coming from in there, wonderful music from a radio or a phonograph, music that's familiar but that I don't remember the name of. I run so that I almost stumble down the path to keep from bursting into tears. I am locked out.

I've walked down numerous steps, and I'm now fleeing down a long street. The houses are getting more modern the farther I go, and the shops are becoming brighter and brighter with lights in the windows and colorful wrappings and arrangements of canned goods. The street finally becomes an open square where the glittering display windows overflow with merchandise and mannequins of both sexes. People—still the same dark people from a southern clime and of another race than mine—turn around and look after me because I'm walking so fast. I want to hide from them, keep walking, get out of sight, and so I just start walking even faster.

But suddenly I stop involuntarily outside a window where one of the female mannequins is wearing the exact same skirt and cardigan that I am.

"So that's where they got my outfit!" I think. I want to go in and ask, because the shop is open, and maybe they speak English in there. I want to know if they remember whom they sold it to or who was with me, because I lost something that day, maybe a letter with an address, and maybe they found it? But at that moment I realize I'm being watched, and I quickly turn around. In a split second, a figure, two figures, a man and a woman, disappear in the shadows under some large trees farther down the street. I don't get a good look at them before they are already in a side street, because other people have come between us. As a matter of fact, others are looking at me as well and probably have been doing so all along because they feel something or other is wrong with me. My face probably looks troubled enough to call attention to itself. But the two figures I saw—or almost saw— turning the corner were different from the others watching me. It's possible that the man is from this place, but I'm certain that the woman's complexion was lighter, although not as fair as mine, and I am positive I felt their glance.

I leave the square and the crowds, walking behind the green booths with refreshments and ice cream at the corner of the square and coming into a street where grass grows between the cobblestones. The street runs between long, low walls crowned with flowering shrubs.

For a moment my feeling of happiness and contentment returns, of the nearness and naturalness of everything, and this feeling is not disturbed when I discover it's the cemetery I'm walking along. On the contrary. I stop at a wrought-iron gate and look in at its little orderly streets with chapels no larger than cakes in comparison to the grandiose style they are built in and with those tall, black cypresses as a background that grow like flames of darkness here and there among the tombs.

I keep walking along the wall, turn a corner, and think I'm on my way toward some new, light-colored apartment complexes that I saw in the moonlight a moment ago through the cemetery gate. But as I get closer, it turns out to be an enormous wall with long vaults of new tombs extending high above the cemetery wall with their empty openings toward me. The cemetery ends here, and I stop for a moment, not knowing what to do, before I decide to follow a glow of light that seems to intensify with a murmur of voices as I approach. I turn one more corner and stop as if paralyzed.

Have I been here before, or is this scene just an image of fear deep within me? Along the back side of the high wall with the tombs, dark clusters of men are staring up those alleys where the light and the voices come from, voices that are now accompanied by screeching phonograph music. Other smaller clusters loiter in front of doors that are bathed in a sick, reddish light and where I see outlines of men coming and going. All the men are waiting for women or for their buddies to come out of the bordellos so they can have their turn. My feet refuse to move, and I feel fear like an ice-cold, drenching rain on my neck and back. I have no idea where to go either. After all, I've just run away from the lighted square at the other end of the cemetery wall and from the mannequin that was standing in the window threatening me and my clothes. I don't dare go past the men. Several of them have already noticed me and are talking about me among themselves. I can see their faces turning toward each other in the ugly, pink light.

Now one person in the distance leaves the group and walks toward me. It's a dark, stocky fellow with an enormous jaw. His teeth gleam white in a grimace that's probably meant to be a smile as he comes closer. Finally my feet obey me, and I rush into the nearest alley, screaming with fear.

I stumble away across the raised cobblestones. The fat, older women with their low-cut tops in the doors and windows, the glossy wallpapers in the background, and the glimpses of mirrors and wall lamps behind portieres and doors flicker past the corner of my eye, as I rush away from this ugly, red, rotten light. I keep running, but finally come to a stop, daring for a moment to look around me.

No one is following me now. But…Again fear constricts my throat so that I must use all the feeble strength in my frail body and in this incredible will of mine to tear myself away again and push on. No one is paying any attention to me either! It may be that the women take a quick look at me, but then they turn to each other again or to those men who are standing at the doors haggling over the price.

Is it because there's nothing strange about a woman rushing down this street with a white, distorted face, which I know it now is? Or is it (Perish the thought!) because they know me and I myself am one of them?

What is this sickening, evil-smelling fear, this dreadful suspicion that took hold of me earlier in the evening? That dark, stocky fellow who came toward me before, smiling…Does he know me? Has he had me—had me—he?

My wounded palms are on fire again, but eventually I realize I'm moving once more and on my way into the alley where it's dark and where I can hide. I walk without thinking about where I'm going, as if I know the way from before and have known all along that I was on my way toward the wide street I see ahead of me now. I walk while the echo of these words in my brain throbs all over my body: Had—had—who has had me? Has anybody ever had me? Yes, I feel it, but who, who?

It's as if I lose consciousness temporarily. But then a strangely liberating sorrow suddenly overwhelms me. I've turned around to make sure that no one is following me, and I walk on up toward the end of the alley, which opens up into what turns out to be a large, dimly lighted square with trees. I walk slowly, thinking of those who have known me and of those whom I don't know, just as I don't know myself and don't know who I am. I feel my eyes brimming with tears, and I can no longer keep from crying. I lean against the wall outside the last house in the alley, while sobbing shakes my frail shoulders. It suddenly seems so unfair for a young woman to be so fragile, as if I had ever had the possibility of wishing for a different gender. I long for someone, just one single individual, who will not follow me, desire me, or spy on me, for someone who will speak kindly to me and call me by name. Maybe by the name that was written on the note: Miriam.

At a closed theater, the life-size posters of a man and a woman taking each other by the hand, seemingly taking leave of each other, mock me from the darkness as I enter the square. Next to the theater there's a camera shop, and I notice in the display window in the light of a street lamp a number of those black and white snapshots that somehow make up your life. I examine them all, straining

my eyes, but not one of them is of me. I also in-
spect the window next to it where larger portraits
are displayed between cameras and rolls of film in
a symmetrical arrangement. A few faces seem
vaguely familiar, but it strikes me that in this symmetrical arrangement one photo is missing: Somehow it's as if the mouth of someone I know is about
to speak to me, and suddenly, unexpectedly, there's
a tooth missing. I keep staring, and I suddenly
know that I've stood here before and that I have
known the person in the missing picture. But in
the spot where it was there's only a void in the direction of the darkness in the shop. A darkness, I
think, and I'm reminded of the high wall with the
tombs, whose squares I originally thought were
apartments because the moonlight confused me,
but which turned out to be just the hollow openings to the burying vaults. I'm also reminded of
the coffin that was brought on board the ship.

I look around the square. In the middle is a tall,
dark monument that I can't see clearly in the dim
light, which makes the square appear hazy, autum-
nal. Behind the façades over on the other side, I

hear the thumping of a large, slow engine. A steam engine.

It thumps in the same rhythm as my heart, but the sound recedes as I walk past a wooden pavilion painted green, where two waiters are in the process of cleaning up under a naked light bulb—walk across the crunchy gravel of the square toward a café that exudes a sleepy yellow light.

I've barely opened the door to the almost empty room all the way before a woman—the same woman who was sitting alone at a table all the way out on the harbor promenade earlier in the evening—calls out:

"Miriam, dear, come on over and sit down! I haven't seen you for ages. Why don't you ever visit old Sheila anymore? How's your arm? Here, let me have a look…"

I don't have the slightest idea who this woman is.

CHAPTER THREE · *Sheila*

I'm on my way up to Sheila's, to that house high on top of one of the cobbled steps that I insisted on accompanying her home to last night before returning to the apartment that I have the key to.

What happened after I stepped into that café last night keeps going through my mind without my understanding it any better. It's like one of those glued-together, constantly repeating films I probably played with as a child, since I seem to know that things like that exist. The film is quite short but, in contrast to this suddenly recollected pastime from my unknown childhood, this film has sound:

The room is yellow, mustard-yellow with a sleepy, yellow light from a large yellow glass ball in the ceiling. Chairs are stacked high right inside the glass door, which I close behind me. At that moment Sheila calls to me.

She is a stocky woman in her forties with large,

listless, gray eyes under heavy, arched brows and with fine lines around them. The straight, medium-length hair that frames her heart-shaped face and encircles her fleshy chin is colored and glistens silvery gray in a bluish shade that becomes more noticeable the closer I get to her table. She has already pulled out a chair for me, and I feel her hand on mine as I sit down. We are alone at the table, and it seems like an eternity while I rack my brain for something to say. I look around the room where a few men are playing chess or talking to each other in low voices in English and probably French and in another language that I don't understand. All the while I feel this strange woman's hand on mine, and I finally turn around with a shudder and look right at her.

She smiles. Her gray eyes observe me with interest and something that approaches friendliness.

"You're awfully pale," she says. "Is it still your nerves?"

I nod, biting my lip to avoid uttering any rash word that might give me away. Now it begins. From now on I must move carefully step by step until the day comes when I know everything.

"Yes," I say. "I'm not doing too well."

"How long has it been now since Anthony left?" Sheila wants to know.

I tremble and struggle just to keep the one hand still that this gray-eyed Sheila in her mauve sweater is holding in hers.

"I don't really know," I say. "Time flies, you know. What day was it now he left?"

Sheila tries to think while absentmindedly squeezing my smarting hand and raising it from the table.

"It was Friday," she says. "The big boat always comes on Friday, you know. Sure, it's only three days ago."

"It seems as if it were yesterday," I say. I stop and hold my breath before continuing, "I must have slept most of the time. I don't have the slightest idea what I've been doing for the last three days."

For a moment Sheila looks at me firmly and quizzically. Then she says as if chasing a thought away:

"I guess not. We haven't seen anything of you at all. It's almost like during that first period when you were lying over there at the clinic."

She makes a slight gesture with her head in the

direction of the wall. Then she takes my arm as if that's what she's been about to do all along and rolls up my sleeve to have a look at my scar.

"Why, it's looking much better!" she says in her cracking, slightly masculine and somewhat tinny voice. "This is a fantastic difference. I mean, it looked awful at first."

"I wonder just how long it has taken for it to heal like that? You know, it's so hard for me to keep track of time here," I say guardedly, looking down at the table so that she won't see my eyes or the blush that I feel rushing to my cheeks.

She doesn't notice anything but keeps turning my arm so that the shiny scar, still reddish and swollen, glistens in the light from the glass ball.

"You're not the only one," she sighs. "It's got to be a couple of months ago. But, of course, it didn't help matters that it had to be broken again, you know. Anthony told me…My goodness!" she suddenly cries. "What have you done to yourself!"

She has discovered the wounds in my palms.

"What did Anthony tell you?" I ask obstinately.

"About your accident. He always said you couldn't tolerate hearing about it…But it's really bad with you!" she moans. "Didn't you bring your pills with you?"

I shake my head, and she gives me a couple of sedatives and calls the waiter who immediately, as if he has had it prepared all along, brings me a large glass of piping hot chamomile tea, which does me a world of good.

Sheila exchanges a few words with the little swarthy waiter in a language that sounds like Italian. I have to control myself so as not to open my mouth and ask.

The next thing that happens is that a tall, blonde girl with her hair gathered in a knot in the back comes in, nods to us, and sits down next to two of the men playing chess. A little later Sheila goes to the rest room, and I use the opportunity to glance down into her beach bag, which she has left behind on her chair. I can see the corner of an envelope peeking out, and without anybody noticing I manage to pull it up so that I can see the name.

"Mrs. Sheila Alcott, General Delivery, La Isla, Spain," it says on it. There is no return address.

When Sheila Alcott returns, the chess game at the other table is over. The tall, blonde girl gets up together with a somewhat older man with a long, narrow, finely chiseled face under an enormous mane of gray hair. They nod briefly in our direction as they leave.

"They almost look like a Wagnerian pair, the two of them," Sheila says in a low voice. "I wonder how long that'll last?"

"Who?" I exclaim, biting my tongue as I say it.

"Wally and Peter, of course," Sheila drones on. "I mean, her name actually is Walfriede, you know." But it wasn't they I meant by my "who," and I'm still biting my lip. My exclamation referred to the young dark fellow with the front lock who had been sitting together with Sheila Alcott at the harbor promenade earlier that evening and who had avoided me when he saw me in front of the kiosk. He was standing right outside and quickly turned his face away when the door opened.

I force myself to meet Sheila's listless, quizzical gaze with a pale smile.

"Yes, you're right," I say. "They really are quite Wagnerian."

I've stopped outside the camera shop. The picture is still missing from its place in the layout.

Through the pane I can see a man standing be-hind the counter straightening some boxes. He doesn't look like a Spaniard, which is apparently what the natives are according to what I learned from the envelope in Sheila Alcott's bag yesterday.

"What about the portrait that was displayed there?" I say a moment later inside the shop. I point to the empty spot while looking into his pale, wa-tery blue eyes which are framed by a broad, non-descript face and curly, colorless hair.

His shapeless mouth begins to smile but straight-ens out again like a mussel that is closing.

"It's been sold," he says in broken English, but his pale eyes look across my left shoulder, trying to hide their curiosity.

"Don't you have another copy—or the negative?" I say, alternately looking around the shop and try-ing to catch his eye. When that happens, he can no longer hide his watery blue smile.

"No, I'm afraid not. Something happened to the negative."

I can feel his smile in my back as I leave. It fol-lows me all the way down the street. It is disgust-ing and transparent and formless like a jellyfish. It has invisible stingers, too; and still I would not hesitate to pick it up if I could only get hold of it—so I would know who I was dealing with inside its abominable, water-colored mass?

The gate to the garden in front of Sheila Alcott's house looks completely different from last night when it was just an iron fence of shadows between swaying branches—and a moaning, all too human sound when it swung on its hinges. Now its pattern of lily-shaped spikes glistens minium red in the sunshine. The pebbles that have been laid in the cement between the beds are blinding white, so white that I don't see the big white dog that is suddenly barking a few feet away from me. I start and clutch my throat.

The dog doesn't bite, but I'm still nauseated with fear when the door to the whitewashed house is opened by a Spanish maid. For some reason or other she seems familiar. She doesn't say anything but smiles at me almost conspiratorially, as if I were in the process of doing something indecent. As I go inside, she remains on the stairs for a moment a little confused, looking at something. I follow her

73

gaze and at first glance see a yellow building higher up, the other side of which must be facing the street leading to the cathedral. Then I discover a long white wall with windows encased in the steep slope just below and a person standing in one of the dark window openings staring over toward us through a pair of binoculars.

It seems to me that I hear the maid sighing when she pushes the door open for the dog and comes in and ties her snow-white apron tighter around her trim figure. She appears carefree, almost frivolous, as she walks ahead of me into the house—over light-colored tiles between plants and mirrors and through an aviary with trees full of colorful chirping birds.

"Have you ever given any thought to what it is that has gradually become the mortal sin of the western world?"

"No."

The "no" is Sheila's. The other voice is that of a tall, gray-haired gentleman with gleaming, gold-rimmed glasses and a clear, wide forehead. His long jacket with a high neck makes him look like a cler-

74

gyman. They are standing in a bright, almost empty room, where sizable enlargements of photographs hang on the walls. One picture is of the explosion of the atomic bomb (How do I know that?). Another is of a little dark man with a mustache. He is wearing riding pants and has a swastika on his arm, and the picture is taken in front of a large old-fashioned car with wire wheels. (That person is familiar, too!) A third picture appears to be of bushes and trees but is actually of enormous crowds gathered in a square. The others I can't see from where I'm standing because of the light.

Sheila waves at me as I sit down behind a large globe, which is sitting in a corner in its stand. The other voice continues. He hasn't seen me but is standing looking out the window toward the houses up above.

"That's 'the mistake.' We *must* be right, and if we aren't, then we must imagine that we are.—In the East they are smarter," he continues. "There they anticipate their ideological defeats by making a cult out of the mistake. They simply experiment their way into the future with the millions of the present, thereby cleverly complying with the desire of the masses for sacrifice—to see someone sacrificed."

His glasses glisten as he turns around. For a moment he looks straight at me. Then he smiles, extends his arms, and comes over and takes both my hands as if he knows me.

"All that old nonsense," he says. "I was just on my way out. It must be these pictures in Mrs. Alcott's bizarre house that always make me go on like this. Just look!" he says, pointing to the nuclear explosion. "We have started to import sunspots, but actually every explosion, and this explosion above all, is a cancer that breaks into our sphere, letting us know that it's ill simply by virtue of the fact that it happens this way and without making it necessary for us to think of all the things that have already happened."

After mumbling these last words, his voice becomes almost inaudible, and for a moment he seems to be lost in his own thoughts. Then he stands up straight and absentmindedly starts spinning the globe.

"It's all wrong to portray our planet like this,"

he says, pointing to it as it rotates from west to east and Asia rushes ahead of Europe and Africa, followed by the empty grid of the ocean and by America's melted hourglass continent (I know them all.)

"No eyes have ever seen it like that, you know. A camera without its victory shirt of clouds." His eyes are completely transfixed now as if he were observing the globe from somewhere all the way out in space. "And maybe that's also what some poor space volunteer will see during his agony or what the divers may glimpse through their thick goggles when they are fighting death and their own nature in the dust heaps of the moon." There is a pause. His eyes are distant. The globe spins faster, turning into stripes of color.

"But human eyes never have seen, nor will they ever see, the Earth like this globe, which actually is just a primitive model of a naive abstraction of this planet, possessing the dimensions of infinity and the realms of dreams and the future, and which only the sick human mind happens to have turned into this grotesque enlargement of the atom that no one has seen and no one ever will see and whose electrons *we* can never become in spite of the efforts of all blind machines."

He stops the globe with his hand on a spot in the Mediterranean. Maybe at this moment his thumb is caressing the place where we are: "La Isla." The little town on the little island that I don't know how and why I've come to. His eyes are still distant.

"What an egregious mistake," he says, standing up straight. "It's already so enormous. And we, we who must not make mistakes!"

I don't dare ask Sheila who he is when he has left after an exuberant leave-taking that made the entire house reverberate with his voice and vibrate with his nervousness. He has obviously seen me before. But Sheila brings up the subject herself:

"It's really too bad about Clement now. It's probably the fear of war, all those rumors of war. He was like that ten years ago when his wife died after they had been married for only three months. That was before he joined the religious order. You know, he used to visit us once in a while in Wales when I myself was very young—before the war."

Sheila shivers, and I sit down on the edge of her chair and involuntarily pull the shawl up around her: *Yes!* I know Sheila, know her perfume and the feeling of her nearness, her shoulders. But how long has that been?

"He can't be that old," I say, adding, "What is his last name?"

Sheila gratefully leans on me, and I feel her hand.

"Gallus," she says. "Clement Gallus. No, we were the same age, and several people tried to get us together when both of us were single again. But I don't think it would have worked, although he's great. There's too much integrity there, you know. Besides, he had too many memories."

I nod. I understand. "What's he doing these days? What's he actually doing here?" I ask, holding my breath. Sheila notices and glances up at me and then out the window in the direction of the white wall on the slope and the big yellow building above.

"I don't really know," she says. "Just what are people doing on this island? He is like a protestant who contrary to his persuasion and reason has landed in purgatory. He talks constantly, talks to everyone here. He has no peace."

Sheila is silent. The birds screech in the aviary. The sun beats down on the town and is refracted in long, shimmering, brilliantly glowing flashes by the swaying eucalyptus trees outside the window. I can see two more large photographs in the room now. One is of the New York skyline (I recognize it!); the other shows a line of dark, half-naked women, young and graceful, wandering along with large jars on their heads. A clock with a deep timbre strikes somewhere in town. I forget to count the strokes.

"It's like that for a lot of people here, you know," Sheila says, "for all of us in a way. We are saddled once more with our worst problems. We act and make decisions one more time—isolated from everything, as we are here."

For a moment it is absolutely still in the house. I can hear Sheila's breathing and my own, and I feel my heart beating. Then the birds screech again. Screech like a pain or like a merciless, penetrating noise that's intended to drown out the pain.

"How can you stand those birds?" I say. I'm starting to like Sheila.

"Oh, you know," she smiles. "I'm a bit deaf—after what happened."

Again this long pause. The birds are silent again as if they have heard her. My blood hums in my ears, spreading an immense space of deafness and emptiness around me, a space with a silent, white sun and with a radiance like white-glowing, molten metal, sending its sparks in and out through undulating shadows. And in the background, in the distance, there are faint, barely visible outlines of coasts and mountains, countries not recorded on any map, oceans and continents where the thought of a planet is merely like a bubble that has burst.—And there are other dark places with fog and smoke and a shadow that never seems to go away, as if there's something between them and the sun. But suddenly the horizon is not there. I see only brightness and drifting clouds, and it gets brighter and brighter, intolerably bright, until a shadow slips across my face again and I realize it's a figure standing over me and then bending over me…

I squeeze Sheila's hand, and she takes hold of mine more firmly. It is as if both of us have been lost in the same regions, because she says:

"You know, it's not easy to be here—on our conditions! People always think it's so easy—endless vacation, holiday, you know what they say."

Sheila has gone in to change. She says we're going out for a spin because the weather is good—it's slightly hazy now under high drifting clouds—and because it's the first time I'm well enough to see the island. I can hear her moving about at the other end of the house. She is struggling with cupboards and pulling out squeaky drawers, and a little while ago I heard a crash and the shattering of glass.

I myself stand bent over a large, disorderly desk in a niche in the large room with the photographs. I notice a copy of the same Spanish newspaper I found in my apartment yesterday, the one with the blurry picture and the headlines starting with "crimen:" Something about a crime. There's a jar of cream wrapped in the thin, yellow paper just like the one I found in "my" apartment. There's also a receipt in English from the camera shop. "One portrait," it says. "Print & negative—Paid."

Just then I hear Sheila's footsteps coming closer, and I quickly steal away from the desk. She is wearing a plain, blue suit with a coordinating scarf that goes well with her light hair. It looks good on her. She smiles at me and gives me a beautiful, lightweight throw to take along on the drive. I can't help returning her smile.

We head for the convertible, which Sheila points out and which I can already see down below in the shade of the trees. As we almost dance, or rather hobble, down the long, gently sloping cobbled stairs with the yard-wide, low steps leading down to the town, I struggle in silence, trying to hold on to these fragile flashes of memory that surround me on all sides but that slip away the moment I reach for them.

We hobble, almost run, down, down some more steps, I with my throw, Sheila with her bag. It's beautiful here; we're between gardens, among fragrant flowers and dark, shady trees. But what is this place? Where is this place? Who am I? And who is Sheila Alcott? Why was I nauseated with fear when I saw the big white dog outside her door? Why do the birds in there remind me of screams and excruciating pain? What is it about this place that everyone knows and only I don't know? And yet, something is coming through. I'm beginning to get a glimmer of something. I know deep down that I've crossed the sea, and the instant I see its vast, bleak, gray surface in front of me, this color that reminds me of Sheila's eyes, there's also a figure sitting in front of me, mesmerizing me with his gaze. I'm weak and can't get away, and the figure holds my hand and doesn't let go of my eyes. He keeps repeating the same words again and again until I, too, say them and continue saying them, till I don't remember any longer…

I want to know. I know I'm being reckless now, but I want to know.

"I'm worried about my passport," I suddenly snap at Sheila as we hobble along.

"Don't be," she says. She doesn't even look at me. "After all, you've got your receipt, don't you? It always takes forever around here."

I remember the note with the hard-to-read "Miriam" and nod.

"Just what do you think of Anthony?" I ask, grateful for the fact that Sheila's sandals clip-clop so she can't hear my heart beating.

But here I'm on dangerous ground. I feel her eyes on me, and I sense a touch of coldness even before I hear it in her voice:

"I guess there's no need for you to ask. You know very well we were all crazy about him. If I've been less than kind to you now and then, I don't imagine you ever had any doubts about the reason for it. We were all envious of you, so let's not hear anything more about that."

I feel dizzy and am just about to fall. But Sheila doesn't notice, because she regrets her outburst right away and puts her arm around my shoulder so that I don't fall.

"I'm sorry, but there's no reason for you to rub salt in an old girl's wounds," she laughs in her shrill voice. The next moment she is about to choke in a violent fit of laughter that immediately turns into a smoker's cough and makes her double up completely. I hang on to her arm to keep from falling, and Sheila takes everything in the best intent, laughing and coughing away. "You're okay. Slap me on the back. You aren't mad at old Sheila, huh?"

Her face has turned purple, and I myself am pale as a doll when we reach the bottom of the steps and see her convertible ahead of us. I wonder why it's black. I look around. No one seems to be watching us. The houses sit like blinding domes of salt in the gardens up the slope, and up above, the cathedral rides on the castle wall like on a gray cloud. I try to muster courage, forget my fear, forget what I've just learned, forget for just a few hours, for just a little while, so that I can make it through the day, forget the grotesque incident a moment ago, forget that I ever asked.

Sheila's normal color has returned. There's the suggestion of an apologetic smile in the lines around her listless eyes, lines that actually are quite attractive. She must be at least forty-five, but she sometimes looks younger. I look at her white throat and feel the soft, firm flesh of her hand, which betrays her senses. I actually think I understand her.

Up on the slope there's a place that looks familiar. I point to it as we are getting into the car.

"Have you ever eaten up there—in the French restaurant? I had dinner there the other night. It was quite good."

Sheila sends me a mocking glance as she starts the car.

"So, Janine has gotten to you, too. Well, I can't say I'm surprised."

We drive out the road I saw from the slope up there in the moonlight last night. We drive between low, gray olive trees, whose black fruits glisten like small, wet stones—or like spying birds' eyes, I think a moment later when a black swarm is frightened and flies up in front of the car, screeching.

Farther out we meet the choirboys in their white lace shirts over black robes. It seems as if it's always the same group that's on the move. They are led by the tall young priest with the frizzy hair, the one I saw down by the harbor. I remember the little twitch of his foot. He greets us in a deep, sonorous voice with a singing "buenos días," which I already know means "hello." Sheila smiles and waves and is forced to shift gears.

"Don Tomás," she says.

I bite my aching lip when he and the boys have disappeared from view. But I've got to say it. I can't help it. I think about a lot of things that blot out others from my memory, but at this moment mostly about Sheila as she sat there alone last night in front of the harbor promenade's outermost bar and later together with the young man who knew me and avoided me when he saw me. The one who was waiting outside the door to the yellow bar around midnight without making himself known.

"Did you see the procession when they brought the coffin down to the ship?" I say. "Wasn't Don Tomás there?"

But Sheila doesn't seem to hear me. She kind of crouches down to look for something below the olive trees, which continue their endless savanna along the road. With bent back she finally points to something, and I, too, crouch down and discern a long, low house with a broad, open courtyard filled with plants way back inside the gray colonnade of trees. Only a narrow, reddish path winds its way to the house.

"What's that?" I ask.

"That's where Henri lives, Henri Lourde. I always have trouble finding it, so I wondered if we had gone past it. But that's the place all right."

"Are we going to visit him?" I ask. Maybe I'm just saying that to conceal the anxiety I'm feeling deep inside this bright afternoon, in the middle of the—in myself.

"He's not the sort of person you just drop in on." Sheila shakes her head. "He's the strangest fellow I know, and it was actually quite by chance that I met him—through Clement Gallus."

"Is he married?" I ask just to say something and maybe because I hope Sheila's weakness will force her to give a funny answer that will make me laugh. But she is serious.

"No, he lives all by himself. Gallus says he was married once, but now he lives alone and hardly sees anyone. Once in a while he'll suddenly pop up in town, but months can go by when you don't see anything of him."

"What does he do? Is he a painter?" I ask. I've already discovered that there are a lot of painters and quite a few writers on the island.

"He may do some writing," Sheila says, shifting gears while still crouching. "He's probably more what you would call a philosopher. He has a strange effect on me. He is friendliness and courtesy itself, but it's as if he can look straight through you so that you begin to feel invisible. It's really odd," she laughs, smoothing her hair while adjusting her scarf with her strong, nicotine-stained fingers. "But that's really how it feels…There—," she calls out, putting on the brakes so that I'm thrown forward and have to hold on—"there he is!"

She points, and I see a tall, slender man with wavy, colorless hair, linen pants, boots, and an old-fashioned lumberjacket, walking on one of the narrow, red paths under the trees. I guess he's got to be in his early forties. He walks easily and nimbly and has not noticed us or the car. Like a hunter without a gun or a dog, I think. It strikes me that that's what he looks like, and I mumble the words to myself: "Like a hunter without a gun and a dog." I have a feeling, a premonition, that someday I'm going to meet this tall, slender man who can make you feel invisible. Sheila has heard what I mumbled. She stares at me in amazement as she starts the car again.

"Without a dog, you say. You know, that's right, that's what I've been thinking, too. It's as if there ought to be a dog."

"Maybe it's become invisible," I venture, "—and the gun, too."

When I have slapped Sheila on the back and taken a sip from her flask while admiring her very appropriate, invisible nail polish, I show her how to shift gears a little less noisily (How would I happen to know how?), and we continue on our way.

The low colonnade of trees continues as far as the eye can see, but here and there the trees are not gray but green and full of fuzzy almond fruits. The horizon rises and sinks in time with the tree tops as we drive, as if the island were sailing, pitching on its voyage: now bright like the white- or blue-plastered houses under the trees, now glistening, gray, new savannas of olive trees.

I see a gypsy family with a beautiful girl in bright-colored clothing taking a siesta under a black fig tree. And not far from Henri Lourde's place near a wide, light path, which Sheila says leads over toward some abandoned mines and to a cave she knows with fantastic stalactite formations, there's a strange, old-fashioned shop by the crossroads run by two women with long pigtails, gold jewelry in their ears, and long skirts above neat, light-colored bast shoes. Time stands still here. We are in another century standing between cupboards with thread and needles and spice jars, and we buy bread, wine, cheese and olives.

When we have eaten, it has suddenly gotten cloudy, and I pull the throw up around me as we drive on.

"Isn't it about time you get yourself some clothes?" Sheila says. "I know Anthony said you lost it all when you had your accident. But fall is coming, and you've got to do something about it, although God only knows the stores don't have much to choose from."

What accident? I don't say anything for a while, for I can't bring myself to ask the question that's on the tip of my tongue. I mustn't give myself away now. I don't know Sheila Alcott. I'm utterly alone and without memory in this unfamiliar place. And something doesn't add up—not about Sheila either, little things, suspicions that I harbor. But I wish I could trust her so that at least I would have one person to talk to. I have tears in my eyes when I say:

"You're right, Sheila. Won't you please help me find the right things? I hope Anthony has left me enough money till he gets back."

I feel Sheila looking at me, and my nails are on their way into my palms again.

"Do you *know* when Anthony is coming back?" she asks sharply.

"No, Sheila," I mumble almost inaudibly. I've never spoken a truer word.

We are approaching a village now. On the outskirts, a butcher is working by the roadside at a primitive table, and skinned goats and lambs hang from the tree above it. In an instant I'm suddenly reminded of something I must have experienced as a child—these sudden flashes (—like when you are giving birth! I think. How do I know about that? I can't have given birth! Or when you are drowning, when you...no!).

Fear has taken hold of me again. I'm trembling with fear, but maybe Sheila thinks it's because of the cold, and she puts an arm around my shoulder and pulls me closer.

"It really has turned cool," she says. "I hope we don't have a storm."

"Why?" I ask a little later.

Again this quick glance and her tinny voice answering, "Oh, no reason."

But I can see her eyes scanning the sea that's in front of us now, as if she is thinking of someone on

93

board a ship, someone who is on his way to the island and whom she doesn't want to tell me about.

The village we are entering is a deserted summer resort with white houses and a low black thicket of firs around a bay. We are alone on the narrow gray beach when we go for a swim; Sheila has brought a bathing suit along for me.

"There's no one here now, but you should see it during the season. It's a war zone," Sheila says.

We lie on the beach for the longest time without uttering a single word. Sheila is reading a well-thumbed thriller that looks as if it has changed hands many times over. The title of it is *Duet of Death*, and the author's face, which is pictured on the back cover, bears a slight resemblance to my own. It's perfectly still where we are, there's not a wave in the lagoon, and I go down and mirror my face in the dark water, comparing it to the other and finding differences.

Sheila doesn't realize what I'm up to. She thinks I'm looking for shells.

"There aren't any here," she calls so loudly that her voice echoes from the other shore. "You can save yourself the trouble. There are lots over on the other side of the island. I'll show you some-day."

Besides, I'm too tired to think. I lie down in the sand and bake in the sun, which has come out again, making the hazy air shimmer across the water. Later on, when it gets cooler and the wind rises, we pack up and walk back between the empty summer restaurants, locked up minigolf courses, and the tall, painted backdrops for the open air nightclubs, backdrops with exotic scenes meant to be seen under floodlights.

We eat on a patio, from where we have a clear view of a kitchen with shining copper pots and pans. The owner, a dark, stocky, well-dressed man with clear, bluish-green eyes comes out and greets Sheila cordially. His name is Magnus—or is it Manuel?—Pantorba, and he also shakes hands with me. But I'm aware that Sheila makes no effort to introduce us.

A fellow by the name of Federico (maybe they use only first names on this island?) with untidy hair and friendly, soup-colored eyes, pinstriped shirt, and a large portfolio under his arm sits down at our table and quickly empties our bottle of wine.

As a small token of gratitude he shows us the contents of his portfolio, which contains sketches that are partly his own work. A series of named caricatures signed "Nickie" stands out—even more so when several of the subjects for the caricatures gradually come in, strike up conversations with Sheila, shake my hand, and sit down at the other tables.

There they sit now: fat, red-haired Tubby with his three double chins, small, intelligent eyes, and incredibly deep tuba voice.—Sasha and Stella, who are sitting in profile just as in the drawing, seem to be rubbing the refined beaks of their race against each other like two birds of a temperament as different as the masks of comedy and tragedy.—Peter, the Wagnerian character, as Sheila calls him, the one I saw in the bar where I met her.—Britta, a young woman with hair like a sulphur-yellow sky, angry eyes, a heavy, squarish face, and a body like a fat baby.—"Tom Two Sticks" with his black canes and his long, bespectacled, sad donkey's head.—Albert and Marylin, he, all nose, monocle, and sports cap; she, older and taller and thinner in reality—in her pink velvet slacks—than in the picture.—But no Anthony. And no me. Me—Miriam?

A guitarist begins to play, and some of the couples start to dance just as Sheila is paying and we are getting ready to leave. Sasha and Stella, who dance past in profile, bump into the chair with the portfolio full of sketches, and when I reach down to help Federico, who is intoxicated by now, pick up the sheets, I recognize on one of them the young man with the lock of hair, the handsome, pointed face, and the slightly drooping shoulders—the one Sheila knows and the one who avoided me. His name is Dave.

As we drive home in the darkness on another, better road and with the top up, I wonder if it was Sheila's intention to look him up in Santa Ana, as the village is called. Or did she maybe want to avoid him and keep him away from me and me from him? And why didn't Federico show us that particular sketch? My thoughts tick slowly like a big old-fashioned clock in this triad, while I look into and up at the darkness where the stars now appear, coming closer, growing larger.

I am shocked to discover the hill of the illuminated town rising in front of me, and I press my hand against my side so that Sheila won't hear the hammering of my aching heart.

It still hurts, hurts worse, when I get my yellow key out and manage to get the door unlocked to "my" apartment, where the roar of the sea comes toward me. I stand for the longest time on the threshold listening but hear only the sea and my heartbeat and my teeth chattering slightly.

Then I turn on the light and notice that the wardrobe is open—or did I leave it open myself? But in the middle of the floor there's a match that wasn't there this morning. And when I walk into the room with the window facing the sea, after having waited and listened for a long time and tried to peek in through the glass windows without touching the lace curtains with my trembling hand, I notice that my bed has been searched. But on the table there's a thick wad of bills with the jar of cream from the bathroom serving as a paperweight.

CHAPTER FOUR · *Faces*

Two more days have passed, and I can't quite keep things straight. Not that anything special has happened. But it's as if everything has come closer. Maybe it's just that I myself am demanding a decision—precisely because I'm afraid of it! Precisely because I tremble with fear of it!—Who am I? Why am I living here?—And who is Anthony? Where is he, and what is my relationship with him?

Everything is like a dream, yet it isn't a dream. I feel thirst and hunger—and, most of all: I'm boundlessly, totally, irrevocably alone. In one's dreams one is actually not so alone. I know that, for I do dream, and I wake up to this other dream, which, I guess, I'm living, and have a vague recollection of escaping and running and of persons that I'm afraid of and that I try to stay clear of because I know them. I also dream about the sea, but at this point I wake up with the roar of the sea in my ears, and the surf breaks a few feet away from me against the foundation of the house.

Here I don't know anyone, and yet: Who is this Anthony? And Dave? And why is he avoiding me? I haven't seen him since that first evening. And where does Sheila fit in?

I have just been sitting for a long time at the barren wooden table, crying in despair. My shoulders tremble, and I cry like a child with burning hot tears, but no one hears me here in the apartment on the sea. The only good it does is that for a while it takes my fear away to be so desperate. I wish I had Sheila for a friend, that I at least had Sheila. But I don't have Sheila.

One of the little things I've discovered since I came back from the drive with her that evening is that Sheila and I have the same maid. She is the one whose name is Maritza, the name on the newspaper in the kitchen that first day. She showed up yesterday morning. I woke up when she knocked at the door, and she looked at me in a strange way and smiled with that knowing smile of hers when I let her in. I don't think she noticed how afraid I was before I realized who she was.

I asked her right away if she was the one who had put the money on the table. At first she misunderstood, thinking I meant she had taken some of the money. There was no end to her torrent of words, which included only a few English expressions. She vigorously shook her head when I got out my yellow key and pointed to her bag to find out if she, too, had one. When I finally made her understand that it was not a question of money that had disappeared but of money I had found in an unexpected place, she breathed a sigh of relief and smiled again her strange, knowing, almost lewd smile, and she showed me on a calendar hanging behind one of the pots in the kitchen that she came only twice a week and that no one had opened up when she came the last time.

When I pointed to the wine bottle and the rest of the packages in the kitchen, she nodded eagerly and yanked new packages and a new bottle out of a basket she had with her. She opened the door out to the stairs to show me she had left the packages out there the last time, and I held on to the kitchen table so that my knuckles turned white to keep her from seeing how this news made me tremble all over. After she had cleaned the apartment and I had gestured to her to run down to buy fruit and a bottle of cognac, I went through her basket to see if there wouldn't be a key after all. There wasn't one, and I could tell that her dress didn't have any pockets either. In addition, she smiled broadly and for the first time innocently when I gave her a generous tip after having paid for the various items she had brought.

So this problem exists together with all the other problems, and I must force myself to stop thinking about them all the time: Who is providing me with money? Who has the key to this apartment? And who would have any interest in keeping me here? (Why did the maid smile in that lewd fashion when she understood I had found money on the table? Why did this strange fear take hold of me when I walked through those terrible streets that first night? Am I—or was I ever a prostitute? I'm sure Maritza is one. I can see it in her face. But what does it mean that I can actually *see* it in her face? That would suggest that I know something about it; in that case I must have been around women like that?) And everything comes back to this: Why am I in this place which seems so far away from all other places? Who am I? And who is Anthony or Tony as Sheila called him just one single time? Is he really gone? Is he the one who is keeping me here? Who, who, who is he? What is it that has happened? What is this accident that Sheila keeps talking about? Who is she anyway? And who am I?

From my window I stare out over the sea and watch the enormous faces of the clouds floating by, dissolving, merging again; some almost dark with anger or passion, some pale as if they were dead or belonged to people who are ill, and some that are like a blinding light in front of the sun so that I can't stand looking at them.

What is this? What is this sea? What is it I see?

The other night I woke up rigid with fear, for it was as if a streak of fire came through the window and the water around the rock that the house is sitting on was like a burning, bubbling pool of molten metal. It took a while before I understood that it had to be phosphorescence, and at that moment it was as if I began to remember something—impossibly far away. But I lost it again.

And yesterday we had a thunderstorm. I kept seeing the flashes of lightning like blackish-violet tracks after they had blinded me. Afterward it poured down, and I couldn't help thinking where and under what circumstances I had worn that raincoat before and the shoes, still earthy and damp, that are sitting in the wardrobe in the other room? And what about the stranger who was here and who left money for me while I was out with Sheila Alcott? What was he looking for in the wardrobe? I'm more and more convinced that that door to the wardrobe was not open when I left the apartment.

I go in to look but don't notice anything different except for the fact that the green theater tickets that were in the pocket of the raincoat before are now crumpled up and lying in the bottom of the wardrobe.

Later I walk over and push a heavy box of table linens in front of the door out to the stairs as a kind of bolt. I did that yesterday, too, before going to bed. But I lay awake for a long time, maybe because it was still lightning. I remember that the lightning looked like hidden springs in a mountain of glass, which suddenly became fluorescent and illuminated everything.

Actually there's a lot of fire everywhere. In the evening the fire basins are aflame in the long street which I'm quite familiar with now, and the boys keep lighting bonfires on the little beach I can see across the bay, just as the fishermen come climbing around the point from the rocks farther out with their fire pots giving off a reddish smoke. I can see them forming a big flickering Z when they come up the trail over there. I also think about it in the morning when the sun glistens in the windows of the strange building up there on the slope where the two figures I saw the first day (the day when something apparently "happened" to me!) often stand looking over toward my windows and turn away again as soon as I look out. (Was it a pair of binoculars that caught the sun over there a little while ago?)

I sit there again looking out over the sea. But all that white out there grows darker and turns to ashes, and when I see a ship on the horizon, I suddenly imagine it's wartime and that other ships with terrible weapons are lurking beyond the horizon. (How do I know that there's something called war and warships? Is that something I've experienced? Am I…?) No, I don't want to think about it, and I look for another prey for my eyes, pausing at the lighthouse, which rises over there at the edge of the tongue of land that frames the harbor.

There's a man who is taken out in a boat in the evening and who goes ashore there. I wonder if it's the same one who has been sitting on the rock below my window fishing, for I've also seen a man being put ashore from the same boat in that spot and disappearing into what I take to be the basement of the house. He didn't look up at me, and I didn't see his face. I hid behind the window casing, but I noticed that the skipper of the motorboat stole a glance up at my window.

Besides I have discovered that two other girls my age live here in the street closest to the sea. Not in the large house where I live—except for my apartment, it seems to be completely empty—but in the small, old-fashioned, plastered houses farther down, which must have deep, dark, cellar-like rooms without light in the interior.

I can see one of the girls when she is getting ready. She washes herself at an old-fashioned washstand with a blue-patterned set on the little terrace she has facing the sea. As a rule she hangs up a sheet, but it blows aside or slips down, and I can see her tanned, naked body and long, flaxen hair, which she forms into a thick braid and then rolls up into a beautiful, high, sort of Chinese topknot. I don't know what her name is, and I don't even know where the entrance to her house is. I think I caught a glimpse of a man just once over on her terrace.

The other girl I have met and talked to, but I don't know her name either. I've seen her a couple of times down in the streets, and I have the impression she's always running—leaning forward with her hands clutching her shoulders, as if she were cold. Her hair is mousy gray, short like mine, but wispy, and she wears black tights and an oversize shirt with fringes, which at first glance look like tatters. Her little tanned face with its sulky, dry mouth, shiny hook nose, and blackish-blue eyes looks gaunt and careworn. She lives in an apartment whose one window out to the alley is always boarded up, an apartment which actually extends in under the large house where I live, and which in a way can be considered one of its cellar regions. I have the impression she has a child living with her, for I sometimes hear yelling and screaming and crying and the sound of spanking from down there.

The last time I saw her she came running or walking in her strange fashion with her arms crossed just as I was about to go up to my apartment. She looked like a bird as she smiled at me with a star of wrinkles around her shiny, tanned nose. She looked at me askance with her ink-blue eyes, quickly glancing back over her shoulder and saying with a voice like that of an adolescent boy:

"Hey, would you mind if I went ahead of you?" She started up the stairs. I followed, and a moment later the tall, pale fellow with the gray cap and the large black book under his arm whom I had seen on the square by the harbor passed by down in the alley.

He stopped farther down and hammered at her door, and it seemed to me that I heard the crying of a child in the background. When he went away again, I turned around and saw a star of cheerless mirth appearing on her tanned face.

"Serves him right!" she screeched in my ear. "By God! It's turned into a real sport!"

I wanted to ask what that was all about, but she had already run down the alley in her flats and stood there sticking the key in the lock as if she were driving a knife into the door.

I don't know what the man in the cap does or what the contents of his book might be. Maybe it's something quite ordinary. And maybe he was the one I heard on the stairs that first day, because the steps seemed too heavy to be the girl's. Or does someone live upstairs after all? The shutters are always closed, but sometimes it sounds as if someone is tossing and turning in his bed at night without being able to find rest. I also heard steps on the stairs another time, late last night when I had pushed the hope chest in front of the door and turned out the light in the outer room. It sounded as if the person were walking with a cane or were lame, and I was reminded of the tall priest with the frizzy hair, the one with the deep, melodic voice whom I've seen a couple of times already leading his flock of choirboys.

I sit again for a while looking out the window. I've just found a note that someone must have pushed under the door while I was taking a bath.

It's from Sheila, and I guess Maritza must have brought it. (That would mean she doesn't have a key then?) Sheila wants to know if I can meet her in an hour in the yellow bar. We are going to a party.

It's protected here, but the sea is white with foam way out beyond the point where a tall column of spray is rising and falling. It looks like snow, a snowscape. I'm no longer thinking of ashes. I'm in a different mood. Instead I catch myself time and again thinking that Sheila is expecting someone to arrive on the island. Someone she doesn't want to talk about. Someone who is maybe already at sea? I think about the fact that it's windy out there, and I don't know why I give it so much thought.

The wind traces long strokes on the sea, long lines like grass and straw and curved reflections of current as if after invisible ships, long strokes that come together to form enormous masks with squares of rippled water and the foam after billions of invisible beings who have never penetrated the membrane of the sea but have perished there and whose remains are now being blown into foam.

I lean out to see if there are large dark fishes as usual, touching the surface with their fins or ring-ing it with their mouths as if they were moving inside a mirror and reflecting someone who is approaching on the other side beyond where the eye can see. But they aren't there today. Only the masks of the sea are spread out in the light, and even the trees and bushes over on the slope form large, angular, staring masks with dark brows in the afternoon light when the sun is setting over there toward the edge.

I look over along the house, down and then up again. All the other shutters are closed, and the other girl's terrace is empty. The only living creatures are the rats scurrying back and forth down by the edge of the rock. I shiver involuntarily and retreat to my room, but the next second my heart stops, for I think I hear someone getting up from the couch in the living room. For an interminable second, a second outside of time, I stand immobile. My body is still, my heart does not beat, for I'm listening while a thousand ice-cold needles prick the nape of my neck and all the way down my spine.

But no one is there. I hear the sound again, but this time it comes from the rock down below where the distant storm is sucking the water out and the return wave rushes in with the metallic sound of a broken spring.

By the time I step out into the alley later on—in a pair of new black slacks and a tight white sweater, which I bought yesterday partly to avoid any hassle with Sheila, partly to annoy her because she is fat and I'm thin and I always feel her eyes resting on me whenever she thinks I'm not looking—I've discovered something else: My hair is colored. It used to be dark—maybe even long? I was sitting in the sunlight in front of the little mirror, which I had placed on the table by the window, combing my hair when I suddenly discovered in the harsh light that the roots had started to turn dark. At first I didn't understand, because the hair everywhere else on my body is not particularly dark, just as I don't have a whole lot of it. But sure enough. My hair was—not black but dark, dark blond!

Needless to say I sat there afterward for several minutes staring into my own questioning, incredulous eyes, which make me confused and shy to start with, trying to imagine how I used to look—and how I maybe actually ought to look?

I don't know what to believe. I cried again, of course, while whispering: Who am I? Who am I? —But it's as if the riddle or the mystery that surrounds me here in this strange place, where I move around in a state of total amnesia, which is like a membrane my mind can't penetrate, is suddenly too great and just makes me tired.

Tired and frightened. Because I sense danger somewhere or other. Maybe in the very fact that I'm here.—Danger in the very fact that I exist, I think, as I turn into the wider alley down below, where I encounter the strange, silent houses with their peeling plaster. Danger in the very nature of existing!—And yet more tired than frightened at the moment. Maybe tired and depressed? Or simply sad, as if I were about to lose something precious.

But what can I lose? For what do I own? What do I have to lose? I have my existence, but what is that? Is it the fact that I sleep and wake up? That I see a reflection of myself in a piece of glass? That I find money in my billfold and can satisfy my needs whenever I feel hungry and thirsty? That I have a bed to sleep in? Is my existence not rather that riddle I am to myself?—and that danger I feel lying in wait for me?—and the hope I'm entertaining? A hope that's directed toward more than a note with a name and an address and a brief explanation! A hope that somewhere down the line, if I'm true to what has been given me to bear, I'll finally find out who I am!

And what I have to bear is the fact that I'm walking around here in this strange place observing all these things around me that are not me.

Maybe they ought to be? I don't know. But in any case they aren't. Here is the street with the old folks emerging from their plastered houses as if it were their tombs they were coming out of in their faded green, dusty black clothes. They have already started tinkering with their fire basins, and some have lighted them so that the smoke drifts through the alley hurting your nose. Inside the houses figures are clearly outlined as they bend over their stoves, while the flames flickering out from under the pots and up the walls make their shadows perform fantastic dances across ceilings and doors. In a couple of hours the last ones will have gathered at the tables around a broken lamp or a candle, as is customary here in the alley. They will slobber down their food while other shadowy beings here and there on the walls carry something invisible to their mouths from the tables of these living beings. And then the day will be over. I've seen them when I come home late. Then they will be standing in the doorways talking, waiting for the cool air that comes toward midnight while a few lamps and bonfires still burn in the street, flickering and smoking when the breeze comes, while the houses remain dark to keep out the insects. And then they will go to bed. You can see them moving about with their candles for a moment behind half-closed shutters, and you can see the flame flickering by their beds while they undress, pulling their sweaters and shirts over their heads and standing in the same position for a few seconds as the large, black cross that hangs above their beds and that looks at that moment like their own shadow.

The next morning it will all start over—like a slumber, a dance. They will go out with their tools. I've seen them on the outskirts of town, hoeing and planting and watering their plants and sowing one thing after another of these images of the will to live, which is actually what all plants are, and whose fruits they will harvest and eat and prepare with such great respect as if they themselves—the workers with their coarse hands and their womenfolk and children—were of less significance than these spindly saplings that reach for the sun and bloom and lose their colored leaves and begin to swell into the shapes they were striving for.

Or they will repair their boats. I've seen them down by the harbor where they dry their nets. They keep their light boats on rollers on a narrow beach below the bulwark of the harbor, which they leave soon after sunset and return home to in the morning with their boats full of silent, shiny fishes and dark eels. Yesterday there were also giant lobsters, slowly and probingly flailing their insect-like limbs—as if, I think, as if all of these things, the boats, the nets, these creatures, were words—about life, about the unspeakable—that had never been expressed but turned into creatures and objects instead.

Objects, days, evenings, mornings. Nights when the individual bodies, when the realms of the sexes merge. (Why do my eyes start to smart now? Why does the lamp up on the wall suddenly widen to form a glittering web? After all, they are not me, these people, and I'm not they, and still I must struggle hard to keep from bursting into tears as I walk on through the alley)…

I'm at the square with the image of the Virgin where the naked electric bulb is burning and where probably hundreds of cats had gathered the other night when I came home late after my ride with Sheila. Now it's the children of the alley that have gathered here. They stand there with their fingers in their mouths, or with open mouths, in their tattered clothes, some of the boys without pants on. Some of the girls have dolls in their hands, and one of the dolls is double, has yet another doll in its hand, as if there were no end to the dimensions of life but everything just reflections and images of images of images of something that might not even be an image itself.—I've had that thought before when I saw them; and now I'm trying hard not to have this thought again, for it sounds like hatred when I formulate it, but maybe it's fear:—What are they doing here? I think. Why the children, too?

(Crazy thought! What do I mean by: the children, too?) I see them standing there in the light of the solitary electric lamp with their almost ball-shaped heads, staring at the icon of the Virgin, which some women are in the process of decorating with flowers again.

Images! I think.—Tiny or chubby or frail or pale or dirty or sniffling images of the images living here in the images of the houses, bearing images, acting in images and being images just like I myself am an image—of what?

I walk around here in the middle of humanity, and I feel I'm a human being like the rest—I think. I've just forgotten where I come from. I've forgotten which image bore and raised me in its image. I've emerged from a great, singing emptiness, and I've forgotten everything that concerns me personally. And yet I carry all those images with me that humanity consists of. Because that's what they call it after all, and that's what I myself must call it, for I don't, they don't, we don't—have any other name for it. Why is it now that I keep muttering this audibly to myself—and repeating it? Why am I looking around so watchfully, almost stealthily, noting all the things I know as if I could acquire them with my words, impress them on my mind— beyond whatever time they have in themselves (— beyond that time I myself have in me) — with my small, dry, oval, stubborn mouth, whose lips I'm moistening with my tongue as I continue to walk and see even more children rushing in the direction of the icon of the Virgin?

I feel lonely. Needless to say. It's almost ridiculous to think such a thought. I'm also scared. Of course, I'm scared! I'm alone, and I feel that I can't trust a single soul here. I obviously know that only too well. Danger is threatening me. Some day someone unknown will stretch out an arm from the unknown that has brought me here. I feel it.

And yet, it's suddenly so immaterial in comparison with my struggle simply to understand *that I'm here*! It's as if I'm wading with long dream-like steps through a lake of reflections.—A shallow lake called "life"; maybe like here: "a street in life" where we live and breed…(What do I know about that? I *have* been with a man. I feel it, and I've examined myself. But who?) live and breed, and those images we breed of ourselves. (Could I be pregnant?

I don't think so. I haven't had my period, but my breasts have become larger and more sensitive in the last few days.)—yes, where those images that we breed of ourselves and that don't grow up and harden until later, as trees harden—where *they* stand, as little girls now stand here with dolls in their hands, staring after us as we walk past; and always one more intently than the others, always one more frequently and longer than the others, like the little dark girl with the straight short hair whose black eyes burn their way into mine every time I walk through the alley. Burn and follow me; burn so that I can't smile at her; burn so that I remember them and keep expecting to meet them in this place where the empty alley ends at the church square. I am relieved when that happens, even if it's painful as well. What I most likely really want deep down is to avoid this totally vulnerable seriousness in these burning eyes of a child.

She, too, has a doll in her hand, darker than she herself. But next to her is another little girl with another doll in her hand, only half the size and white as dough. And in the dim light between the trees in the church square, the boys run around with their hoops. I can hear them before I see them. I guess they always do this at dusk now when the street lights come on here—just as surely as tomorrow around noon they will be sitting in the sun burning celluloid with a speck of sun no larger than the head of a pin; while the older boys throw coins at a line they have traced in the mud, coins which it is customary here for boys to buff to a high polish and which glisten drowsily up at me yellow and white with their rubbed-out profiles when I walk past at that hour.

Now the girls sit down with their dolls in the lamplight on the balustrade over in front of the shop where I bought fruit yesterday. This is also where the young woman with the long braid down her back for every customer she has must work hard to get her thick red fingers down into the jelly glass where she keeps her money.—The dolls must go to sleep, everyone must go to sleep soon. The light has the same color on the horizon as the large, pale, violet globes I can make out now down by the harbor. The woman with the dogs walks past at the outer edge of the square. She doesn't notice me, neither does she notice the tall, gray man with the cap and the book. But the woman without legs in the wheelchair looks after me. She has stopped to chat with her girlfriend, whom I call "the one with the pain." She never looks at anyone. Her head moves from side to side, her one hand pressed against her abdomen while the fingers of her other hand move up and down the outstretched arm as she plays the deep, inaudible scale of her pain.

I'm afraid of pain. I must have felt quite a bit of it because of my arm (which Sheila says had to be "reset." Why didn't she answer when I happened to mention it again the other day?) I wonder if they have given me an overdose of drugs? I have an enormous, dry hunger for something somewhere inside me. I don't know for what?

The large clumsy building down by the harbor, the one that looks like an overgrown desk set, is a bank. The light is on in some of the windows, and I can read the word "Banco" in the frosted glass panes. They must be open at night, for there are customers at the counter inside. Now one of them is bending down to count a stack of bills. It's Dave—with the lock down his forehead.

When he comes out, I follow him unobserved, and we arrive, he with a considerable head start, at the café where I met Sheila the other night and where I'm supposed to meet her again. But he has disappeared when I step inside—presumably through a back door.

He is still not there ten minutes later when Sheila arrives, and we leave immediately and head for the waiting, old-fashioned cabs with most of the other guests from the café.

It's like being in a garden. I'm surrounded by shrubs on all sides, but the leaves are faces.

I'm slightly drunk, for Sheila keeps filling my glass. We are upstairs in a kind of mansion, a large patrician house where the bishops of the island once lived, she says.

The faces keep appearing and disappearing. They turn away, becoming almost invisible and then appearing again. It's as if a breeze wafts through the bushes. Or like when you're dreaming: Faces I have only glimpsed, faces that I didn't know until just a moment ago, are familiar to me already now, surrounding me on all sides in this undulating crowd.

The ceilings are high, the walls far away. It is halls we are sitting in. There's hardly a stick of furniture. We sit on mats and pillows along the walls which are covered with paintings and occasional photographs and prints, some of which seem vaguely familiar. But now that I'm drinking wine, now tonight when I'm here in these empty rooms high above the town, they all mean something else, something inexplicable and clandestine that becomes a part of my intoxication.

It's also as if I've been here before. But maybe that's only my imagination, or if not, it goes back to a movie I once saw in the town where I lived then (Lived! Lived?).

The main entrance must be blocked. You reach the mansion through a slum with narrow streets without courtyards behind them like the ones you see farther down in the town. This is why the laundry up here is hung out to dry in the streets themselves so that you have to stoop under it or push the tattered sheets aside with your hand, as if you're fighting your way forward in a snow squall. (Again this recollection of snow!)

Then suddenly, through a beautiful, pillared door

that's almost eaten away with age in a peeling wall, you step into a courtyard, where there are enormous clay pots with dying trees in them. The courtyard is covered with a worthless, wild-growing canopy of vines creeping in across the wall from a garden on the other side. In the middle of the courtyard there's a lion fountain, but it's dry and cracked, and the lions lack either heads or paws or noses and stand there like a forgotten monument to life and times that are long since past.

We have all come through this courtyard except for those who live in the house, which has several apartments now. We have walked up the chipped marble stairs to the mansion, across the light, patterned tile floors, large areas of which have cracked here and there baring the bricks underneath. Some areas have already turned shiny from being walked on.

I move from group to group, and the shrub with the faces recedes, flashing into invisibility like leaves that suddenly turn their sharp edges toward me, flashing and becoming visible again. There must have been about a hundred people here tonight. Some have left, and some are about to leave,

but those who are still here look as if they are determined to go on all night.

Take Blond Pete, for example, in whose honor
the party is being given. He's taking a trip, they
say. (I wonder if they'll also throw a party for me
the day I leave? [Where to?] It seems to be what
they do around here!) He sits there like a pope in
the only armchair in the room, a leather chair that
is low and worn. He is wearing square, horn-
rimmed glasses, and his round, short-haired, sunburned owl's head has hair that is so sparse and so
light that it looks white. He and everyone around
him have a glass in their hands, and so do I. On the
broken arm of the chair sits Ruth Sherman with
her lilac glasses on. She is wearing a striped camp
shirt, and her white, bony knees and dark, hairy
legs are farther out of her skirt than she realizes.

Ruth Sherman. I've begun to learn the names
and even to remember them—even though I've had
a little too much to drink. I usually remember only
first names, for they use first names here, and it's
usually just first names you hear. But Ruth
Sherman is the kind of woman you automatically
would call "Miss Sherman" and expect to see come

running with a steno pad in her hand. For the time being it's a glass she is holding, and she has her arm around the waist of Blond Pete, the one who is taking a trip. Her thighs are almost bare now, and Blond Pete has lipstick in his white hair, but even so you would never think of applying the word "erotic" to this scene. Because of Miss Sherman.

"Paco!" she calls out, "play something else! Why did you stop?"

But Paco, who is so Spanish black in his black clothes and black tie and with his black hair and black eyes and black sideburns that he is blacker than any black you could think of, just in a different way, he simply shakes his head and puts his guitar away in its black box. Then Rudy, a young man in color-splattered linen pants, a roundhead of the same type as Pete, shouts through the din:

"There's no point in asking him, Ruth. You know very well that Paco only plays if it's quiet."

A high, screechy voice interjects:

"Yeah, his own bar is like a damn temple in that regard. You can hardly get up the nerve to drink the wine he's serving. In any case, it's not nearly as good as this. Cheers!"

It's Nickie Brown, the caricature artist, a red-cheeked little fellow with a bobbing, pointed beard and a beret to hide the complete absence of hair on his head. He sometimes jumps up as an indication of sheer vitality—straight up in the air from the mat where he sits leaning against his fat wife, Annie. She shows her slightly protruding front teeth now as she slaps his fingers because the wine from his glass splashes on her. Sighing and smiling and sucking her teeth, she looks so perfectly happy that I wonder for a moment if in spite of what has been said this evening for and against this particular subject—it was Sheila who brought it up a couple of hours ago; I think she couldn't quite figure out what she herself thought about it!—if it wouldn't after all be heavenly bliss for a woman to be married to a fawn.

Her hair is like dark, tarnished copper. It's the most beautiful head of hair I've seen on a young woman this evening. (I keep wondering how my own hair used to look.)

Incidentally, Nickie is surrounded by the subjects of his caricatures.

Drying an invisible drop from her nose with the

edge of her glass, Ruth shouts with her narrow lips:

"It was Ted who ruined everything. He always wants to argue. Pete *loves* Paco's music, and it's his last night."

Ted has just been out taking a shower. He's sitting like a Buddha on his mat, wearing nothing but a loincloth. He looks like a Buddha, and he smiles like a Buddha, but he is certainly no Buddha. I saw how he furtively tried to assume the lotus position when he came in. Now he's sitting there rubbing his ankle. Whatever, he is a great cook, Sheila says. He has gotten involved in a discussion about art:

"Nonfigurative art," he says, scratching his navel, "simply means you've got so close that you stand there like a nearsighted person staring at a wall or a weldment."

Ruth hasn't heard a thing.

"I just love impressionism," she says. "It's just like a morning in Paris with haze and sun and smoke in the air, a winter morning in Paris, when I was—"

"—young!" says Maurice who is sitting in a prison-striped shirt on the floor next to her. Roaring laughter. Ruth blushes visibly, which makes her lilac glasses look weird. Maurice doesn't move an inch of his frail, slumped figure nor a muscle in his expressionless face. His lips are thick, and his large, melancholy eyes are heavy and arched. When he comes to a complete stop, they sometimes look as if they were ready to fall out of his head without his being aware of it. Then it seems as if he is doped or hypnotized. In a way he isn't really a caricature like the rest. I look around the circle and catch myself thinking that the others are from the past just like me but that Maurice—well, he's from the future! Crazy thought, but there's something to it. It's as if he isn't really present here—yet. And it's as if it's his concern about the fact that someday he will be present that casts him into this endless melancholy.

Now Ted's jovial voice can be heard. He has found something in his navel and is sitting there contemplating it on his nail:

"You might also say it's like frosted windows through which you keep trying in vain to look out in a street—"

"—which no one can paint any longer because it

doesn't exist!" answers the deep tuba voice of Tubby.

"He's great, wish he would continue. But he isn't feeling too hot tonight. He's sick—." It's Sheila who is suddenly behind me. "When he starts to say something, it always gets deathly quiet. He's a disabled veteran. It's his mind," she whispers. "You know."

It *is* deathly quiet for a moment. Red-haired Tubby, who is sitting on a footstool leaning against the wall with his black cane in his hand, slowly turns his massive, blotchy, heavily perspiring head, which must weigh a ton, toward Sheila but doesn't say anything.

"Tubby is always so full of paradoxes!" Nickie screeches, jumping up and down on his mat. "My God, the other day he insisted we were not on 'La Isla' but somewhere outside of history. And there aren't too many islands that have as much of a history as 'La Isla'—except for the bit of history we ourselves dream up."

He laughs like a horse, downing the contents of his glass.

Sheila nudges me, and I follow the direction of

her glance.

On the floor in the middle of the circle sits a tall, angular figure with an unruly, blond head of hair. A couple of thick wisps hang down over the blue turtleneck he is wearing. I've seen him a couple of times on the street down in the town—just as I've seen all the others before who are here in the room. After all, the town is not that large. But I don't know his name. I call him "the guy in the blue sweater." He is sitting with his hands around his knees, his narrow, bony feet halfway out of his brown, laced shoes, whose backs he has worn down in order to use them as slippers. His blue linen pants are painted yellow with strange childlike drawings on them.

"He has the boys paint those on him when he walks around down in the town. He always carries a crayon for that purpose. No doubt about what he is, huh?" Sheila whispers.

I nod. The conversation drones on. I hear Ruth's voice. Her sentences always start with: "It's one of that kind of…that sort of…that type of…It's just like, you know…"—as if everything can be found in an enormous library which Ruth Sherman has access to and where she herself can be found as well: Ruth Sherman from New York's jagged chain of window-perforated peaks, the way they are portrayed in the large photograph at Sheila's house. (Still this: How do I know it's New York? Am I American? Or did I just visit that country once?).

Blond Pete, who is going on a trip, has torn himself away from Ruth Sherman's demonstrative embraces and is now drying off her childish kisses with a large handkerchief with red dots. Trying to bring the conversation they have had to a close, or talking as if he means something totally different with his remarks, something that only he himself knows, he says:

"Art—maybe it's quite simple to understand art. I mean, it originates somewhere before we are born. It comes from what is not yet created, from the possibilities of creation before destiny and before existence."

"Sure, but now everything is present," Tubby growls, perspiring hard and tapping his cane on the floor.

"Yes," says Blond Pete, looking at him for a moment without his glasses on and with a peculiarly direct gaze that I had no idea he had at all. "Yes," he says, "everything! Only we are not."

It's perfectly quiet for a moment. Tubby collapses as if the other fellow had put a knife in him. I suddenly notice the Japanese couple that I've seen down in the streets quite a few times. They have been sitting behind Tubby all the time without saying a word. They sit there immobile as if they hear and grasp everything.

Sheila is restless. She is standing over by the window now, looking out over the town and the harbor. Again I follow the direction of her gray eyes, and I see some lights moving down by the water. It could be a little boat that is just coming in, but I can't be sure.

Now Sheila is over by the window at the opposite end of the hall. She comes back saying:

"I see a cab down there. I'm just going to run out and pick up something. You wouldn't happen to have any money? I forgot my billfold."

Now I've got my chance. I look straight into her eyes to see what will happen as I say:

"No, Sheila, I haven't got a penny tonight—not here and not back in my apartment either. I mustn't forget to go to the bank tomorrow morning to cash a check."

No surprise on her part. No wrinkle on her brow. Just a nervous smile that isn't meant for me. Just the distant look in her gray eyes and the voice saying kind of to itself:

"Never mind! I can pay him later. I've got to run. Bye, bye."

She kisses me on the cheek and disappears. I hear her heels clip-clop down the wide, chipped steps.

I'm left behind with my finger on my cheek, knowing that it's not Sheila who is providing me with money; but at the same time I realize more than ever that she is hiding something from me.

When I return to the group, everyone is sitting there talking about the trees in Canada.

"If they didn't keep an eye on the forests over there," Rudy says boastfully, "they would gradually invade and cover the cities. You ought to see the big trees. They are so enormous that ten men can't span them."

I meander over to the other group in another corner of the hall. There my "neighbors" are sitting, whose names I've finally learned

The little one with the dustmop-hair and the fringe-sleeves, the one who always walks or rather runs leaning forward and who's sitting here now, too, leaning forward with her arms crossed and her hands on her shoulders as if she were cold, that's Cora.

The other one, whom I've seen only from the distance over on her little terrace when she washes herself and combs her long hair, that's Doreen. She's still all body and hair.

Peter Holm is presiding in this corner together with Wally—who really looks as if her name were Walfriede; Sheila is right! Just a minute ago, intoxicated by the wine, he pawed all the girls in the group at the same time. He had that triumphant feeling that he resembled the classic ideal of a man, and Cora latched on to him like a leech, which he had to remove from his body with force afterward. Doreen with her light-colored eyes, tanned skin, and long colorless hair the same shade as her teeth didn't seem to realize what was going on. In one way she looks like the negative of a picture. In another she makes me think of a well-preserved mummy from Nordic antiquity, of a woman with long hair and wearing a bast skirt, that I must have seen at one time or other. A mummy that's been brought back to life again, a—what's the word now? (And how did I ever hear it?) A zombie. She is just *there* without really being present and in a state of melancholy that's just as deep and which has the same cause as Maurice's, who has also come over here and plopped down next to her. The only difference is that she is totally and completely unaware of everything other than the fact that the men will fondle her and she'll let them.

Peter Holm is a "tachist," an "action painter." Sheila told me. His clothes are stained with paint, and he has paint in his eyebrows and his hair, for he paints by throwing the paint on the canvas as when you smash an egg. One of his paintings hangs here on the wall, and it could be anything. You can read all kinds of things into it, just as you can in an inkblot or in an old, damp, cracked wall. But what you can read from a wall usually has been in the making over a long period of time. It has shapes, maybe it forms figures, frequently as in your dreams or those myths you remember, (Remember?) and these figures seem to be part of the wall and to tell something about it alone.

Here there's no form, just chaos. I stare at the picture, and it strikes me that it mostly looks like a beach with thousands and thousands of human beings. In any case, an enormous gathering of people in a playing field or in a city, the way you would view it through a pair of binoculars if you…if you were in the process of…in the process of throwing a bomb in their direction. (Why am I trembling now? What is it that I almost remember?).

There are more girls in the bouquet Peter Holm squeezed against his color-stained, almost parodically well-proportioned person. (Am I envious? I would deny it, but I still feel this dry hunger for something I don't know what is). Two more pairs of girls. The girls seem to come in pairs on this island. (Sheila and Miriam? I almost smile, then bite my lip and sit down all by myself, shaking my head).

One such pair is Diana and Ingrid. Diana could be one of the native girls with their voluptuous figures and long braids. You wouldn't be able to tell the difference if she dressed the way they do and did what they do. The shape and the braid she has got all right, and the latter is even longer and thicker and shinier than those you see around here. But that's where the comparison ends because her face has heavy eyelids and heavy features which—like her dark, cunning eyes—all speak of an unhealthy sensuality that has taken possession of her entire person. You can tell it has already made her a calculating player for her sex, which will soon make her body swell into grotesque shapes, scaring the men away and leaving her behind in pain.

She could hardly be more than nineteen years old, probably only seventeen or eighteen. Everything about her is heavy—her walk, her hair, the way she sits—and her heavy breasts are tied up in a man's shirt with a thick, tight knot above her bare midriff. You can even tell she is one of these women who must wash constantly so as not to fill all the rooms they walk through with that penetrating odor that's a part of their nature and person.

Ingrid is her opposite. Here sensuality is burning dry, present in every pore of her tanned skin, which is stretched smoothly over her cheeks and the bones of her hands. Ingrid is fair; she is from one of the Scandinavian countries. Her blue eyes have the color of the blue sky; it's as if you can look straight through her out into a clear blue day.

I myself have blue eyes, too, and I wonder for a moment if I, too, might be from one of the Nordic countries? Maybe my family is from there? And yet my language is English, isn't it? Or do I merely come from a place where they mostly speak English—like here? And has my shock, my loss of memory, whatever it may be, blocked the sources of an entire language from me? I can't believe it, don't want to believe it. After all, I do find Americanisms in my speech that seem to indicate that I've lived in America for a while or that I've been around Americans. I recognize occasional French and Italian words in the conversations I hear. But no other languages.

And then there's something else about Ingrid: She is of another race—without my knowing what I mean by the word "race." She is *different*. For example, her wrinkles, and she has many—from having been a young girl for at least twenty years and from lying on beaches and squinting in the sun and smiling at the other sex—her wrinkles run in a pattern completely different from that of other people.

I catch her eye as she sits there quiet, completely passive, with her smooth hands in her lap in an interval between bath and bed and meal; and it's as if I look into a different, cooler, emptier part of the planet through her eyes.

"Ingrid," I ask. "What nationality are you actually?"

"Swedish," Ingrid answers, looking at me unruffled with eyes from the northeast, while all faces turn toward us for a second, as if wondering why I would be stupid enough to ask about something that obvious.

Another pair is Katy and Louisa. They are completely different. They are pale as if they never see the light of day. Their skin is white and soft, so soft that, now that I'm looking at them up close and not just down in the streets or in the cafés, I automatically and a bit shamefully touch my own, which is soft, too, only not like theirs.

Katy is slender and frail, completely in black with bare arms and a low-cut top. Louisa is her reflection, only that she, as the tone and sound of her name suggests, is more voluptuous, a bit blonder with her long hair high on her head. There are gold threads in her dark dress with its rustling skirt over her slender legs, and she is wearing gold slippers just like Katy's. Both of them wear eye makeup only, which frames their eyes and makes their gaze staring and unreal, as if their respectively gray and gray-green pairs of eyes were no longer intended to see with but merely to be seen.

They are feminine, these two women, as feminine as can be, there's no denying it. But I can feel they are bringing a problem with them that must have plagued me sometime already in my unknown past: I'm a woman, too. I'm feminine, too, at least I hope so, and I think so. I can blush all over and begin to think with my body; I can be affected by its throbbing and the tingling of my nerves, while my eyes grow distant and I'm drawn toward a man as toward a mountain or a forest. No doubt about it.

But I'm not like those women who have practically made themselves objects of femininity and sacrificed everything for it. I feel that they, too, are strangers, that they, too, have come into existence after…(After what? Just what kind of thought is this that keeps haunting me without ever having a conclusion or becoming totally clear?)

Maybe they, too, feel like outsiders at this moment? They have been sitting there for a long time without saying anything, and now they are getting up to leave, briefly nodding goodbye to Sasha and Stella, the handsome Jewish couple I saw for the first time out in Santa Ana when I was there with Sheila. It's as if they always sit like birds in profile to each other, one of them in deep melancholy, the other with her mind steaming like a dark oven with the high spirits that are keeping the other one alive.

Katy and Louisa gather their skirts around them and disappear into one of the other rooms of the old mansion. They have a beautiful walk. My gaze follows them out of the room.

A moment later a new group of people is chatting and gesticulating where the girls were sitting. It's the gray-haired Swedish woman that everyone calls Mama and her large, strangely baby-like daughter, Britta, who have arrived in the company of Federico, who as always has the portfolio with

143

his sketches under his arm, and another swarthy fellow by the name of Mustapha.

I smile at the thought that Federico can move in all circles with this giant admission ticket under his arm. The two women apparently have come out of curiosity. They don't fit in here, and just now I hear them explaining in unison that it was Federico who invited them to come along.

Actually the dark man, Mustapha, has come to pick up Ingrid, and she obediently gets up and follows the group when it moves on again. The last I see of them is Federico who is throwing kisses back over his shoulder. They seem to be meant for Diana, but it's just possible that I'm included, too. After all, I'm also one of the girls in town, and maybe he thinks he knows me after I asked him yesterday if I could have a look at his portfolio and leafed through it hunting for that sketch of Dave.

It wasn't there.

And Dave is not here. Apparently everyone else is or has been here in the old mansion tonight. All the faces in town. But not Dave.

I sit here thinking about him, his gangly figure, his particular walk, his lock of hair falling forward;

and I wonder where Sheila might be now that I realize that another late guest has arrived and that that person is sitting there watching me.

It's a woman. She is short, red-haired, and has golden eyes. She smiles at me.

I look into her eyes, which suddenly seem coal-black when her face is in the dark and in strange contrast to her red hair. My gaze moves down over her finely lined neck and her narrow shoulders in that luscious silk shirt, down to her tight black jeans—which are too snug for her—and her long, manicured hands, resting in her lap. I look for a long time at her hands before meeting her gaze again. On each of them, one finger is a little thicker than the rest, and she is wearing a large ring to conceal the fact.

I've seen her before. I just don't know where. We must also have spoken to each other, for she smiles again and addresses me in English:

"It's late," she says.

I nod.

"I never can go to sleep when they are partying up here," she continues. "I live in one of the apartments downstairs. In the nether regions of the mansion," she says, smiling again without moving her body or her hands. She has a nice smile, and she sticks her tongue all the way out between her teeth when she smiles.

"You can hear every sound," she continues, "and besides there's a crack in the wall down there where sand falls out once in a while when they dance up here. Actually it has made it almost impossible for me to hire any help."

"Why is that?" I ask, although I know the reason very well.

"Because they are superstitious."

I nod. "What is your name now? I remember your face, but not …"

"I'm Nora," she says, crossing her tricot-covered legs. "But I haven't forgotten that your name is Miriam."

My hands spread out. I apologize. "I'm so forgetful," I say. "It's so hard for me to remember."

Now she chuckles, her tongue sticking out again between her thick lips.

"Sometimes that can be a decided advantage," she says cheerfully. "I myself seem to remember only too well and too long."

146

At that moment both Blond Pete with his glasses on and Ted in his loincloth come by on their way out with empty bottles. They squeeze her from both sides.

"Hi, Nora, nice to see you," Ted says.

"Won't you join us for a drink," both of them say simultaneously.

"In a while," Nora nods while I struggle with this stinging feeling of being an outsider, of being different from the rest, a feeling of shame and cheap resentment at not being the one who's asked.

I wonder why. What is it about me?

Sasha has turned his profile away from Stella for a moment. He is sitting there, watching Peter Holm's action painting on the wall above him, which, I notice now, is hanging next to one of Walfriede's drawings, the ones she signs "Wally." She always draws the same thing: herself. And always in the same way. It's a kind of composition with a beach and a huge turned-away woman's head reaching all the way up toward the clouds like a rock, while the body disappears in the sea.

"Just what did you have in mind when you painted that, Peter?" Sasha wants to know. His face is flushed with friendliness and interest, and at this particular moment he is innocently concentrating on this one problem.

"Peter never talks about his work, not even to me," Wally says bitterly, turning her face away. The drawing is accurate. It looks like her.

With her face still turned away as if she were trying to catch a glimpse of a ship…(A ship! A ship? What is it that is happening…?) a ship invisible to the rest far away on the ocean she has sunk into, she continues:

"He only talks about the time when he was a clown."

"Well, why not?" Peter Holm laughs, his mouth flashing with gold. He slaps his thighs while rocking back and forth, and his hair falls forward across his forehead like the horns of a ram. "That was my best time."—"When was your best time, old Wally?" he continues, slapping her back hard and encouragingly a couple of times.

"You ought to know." She slowly turns her face around toward him, slowly as if it were against her nature. "That was when you modeled me in the yellow clay from out there by the caves, you know—inside the caves!" She smiles. It's her evening tonight. Her triumph.

"That just goes to prove that Peter has got a screw lose if he is using that clay. The red stuff from the beach way out there is much better. I'll be happy to show you someday, Peter!"

Cora's narrow mouth has already closed again. It remains silent and thin as a slit until the laughter has subsided. Then it spews forth again:

"I know what that picture is all about, for I know Peter better than he knows himself. It's *death*. There was such an atmosphere of death in town that day. I asked Peter if he wanted me to crawl through the color for him to inspire him. I've done that before. He always says it reminds him of all the places he has been with a woman out in the open. But that day he didn't want to hear of it. He said something dark was pressing against his temples trying to make contact with him, and the next day they found the man who plunged from the rock lying dead on the little beach I can see from my room. They say it was murder."

Her mouth is a slit again, and I realize to my horror that I can't help speaking up myself.

"Was he the one that was brought on board the ship in a coffin…which the procession accompanied down there?" I hear myself saying. "I forget when that was," I continue.

"But that's only a couple of days ago. I remember," Nora laughs. Her face is in the light now, and her eyes are golden. She gets up and walks over to the other group from where Ted and Pete and even Tubby keep calling her.

I nod to myself, for she is quite right. It's only a couple of days ago that I saw that coffin, and maybe there's no connection with me whatsoever, with my situation. I mean, it's only a few days ago that I woke up and discovered I was *here*.—When was it Sheila said that Anthony left? He left on "the big boat," she said, the one that will be back tomorrow. So it's been six days since Anthony left, "my Anthony," as Sheila says. I wish I could ask one of the others if they have seen Anthony? Can't I ask them if they saw Anthony leave? Or can I?—No. Impossible. After all, the question that's burning on my lips is: Who, who, who is Anthony? And…

I knock over a glass as I get up, and for a moment everyone looks in my direction. I must move around to prevent my emotions from getting the better of me…

Without my knowing it, I've already made it into another room where there are some wine barrels, small and large ones mixed. People are sitting on most of the small barrels, and two men are leaning against the largest one.

"…only 10,000 years since the last ice age ended…," I hear. "…only 25,000 years since it began…," the voice continues.

"Sure, but it's even closer," the other fellow answers. "You're forgetting that the ice cap at the South Pole began to form only 6000 years ago, at the time of the Pharaohs. And if you'd just imagine for a moment…"

"Miriam!" a woman's voice suddenly calls out. "Miriam, do come over here and sit down by me."

The voice belongs to a tall young woman, tanned, with short, dark, frizzy hair and dressed in a youthful plaid dress with a belt.

I look at her face. Do I know her? Do I know this open, friendly, but kind of sleep-struck face with the radiant eyes, the right one of which is so fixed and different from the other that it looks as if she were wearing a monocle?

"Rebecca was just asking about you!" a man's voice now says.

I start and notice that it's the slender, dandyish gentleman with the powdered face who always greets me so exuberantly on the street and whom I suspected of following me one day. Next to him is the photographer with the shapeless mouth. He is trying in vain to put it into a position that looks like a smile.

Suddenly I'm completely still and cold with fear. I don't know why. I feel I shouldn't have gone into this room. But Rebecca, as she's called, whom I guess I must have met before, is friendliness itself. She pulls me aside and breathes an audible sigh of relief when we are out of earshot.

"Didn't you get the message I sent the other day? Maritza must have forgotten. You know, my parents were here, and I know a lot of older people whom I have to invite for tea once in a while. It was supposed to be today, but it was postponed. Now I have changed it till tomorrow afternoon at Sheila's; she has more room. I ran into her just as she was leaving, and everything is arranged."

She is completely breathless. Her right eye shines at me—with eagerness? Or is it fear? Maybe she really likes me. She is the only one who has called to me and really taken notice of me tonight—except for Sheila, of course. But Sheila is weird.

"You will come, won't you? Promise me you'll come, then it won't be so bad, and then we'll get it over with in a hurry. Promise me you'll come, Miriam!"

I nod in agreement. One more party, more faces to search among. Why not? I like Rebecca. But precisely for that reason I've got to be on my guard. Why is she sitting here with these men whom I mistrust, who may be following me, and who I feel—indeed know—I can't trust.

I make it a point not to look at the photographer, but nod in the direction of the slender, dandyish man with the long, powdered face.

"Who is that?" I ask.

"Oh, him," Rebecca blushes a bit. "Don't you know him? You must have seen him at—well, never mind. He is really polite, you know, attentive. He is an antique dealer. I think he was a civil servant at one time. His name is Rafael Vega."

"What kind of civil servant?" I try to make my voice as natural as possible.

Rebecca runs her long, tanned fingers through her hair. Her nails are painted a pale blue to match her eyes. She looks around perplexed. Her "monocle" glistens. It's as if her eye is directed at a shiny flying point way out in space.

"They say he was chief of police here on the island," she answers reluctantly. "But people say all sorts of things, you know. The others over there you know, right? That's Stan and Dick."

I look in the direction of Stan and Dick, a short, ashen man with yellow eyes and a large, tanned fellow with brown ones, two men who have found a bar or something that resembles a bar, and something to talk about at that bar. They are still discussing ice ages and polar caps and what will happen to them, to the polar caps, if...

Rebecca takes my arm: "Get a load of the Japanese over there!"

I turn around. Indeed, she's right. The Japanese have come in here, too, and are sitting in a dark corner.

"They pop up everywhere," she whispers. "No

matter where you go, there they are. They never say anything, but you know something? I've got a sneaking suspicion that someday they will suddenly open their mouths and repeat everything they have heard down to the last detail."

She giggles and runs her fingers through her hair, and I can't help laughing with her.

"But then what about them?" I say, motioning with my elbow to two short-haired girls in wind jackets and slacks, who are holding hands but sitting in a corner saying nothing.

"That's Frankie and Leslie," Rebecca bursts out laughing. Her hands flail in front of her. "That's a completely different story. They are just the way unmarried aunts always have been. You know, these aunts who surprise you with their knowledge of life even though they themselves have never lived it. Here you see them in their youth!" Rebecca's eyes shine triumphantly at me. "They are just dressed differently. Could you imagine Frankie and Leslie in high-necked lace blouses?!" She doubles up with laughter, burying her face in my shoulder.—I suddenly feel like tousling her hair and kissing her cheek. Is there something wrong with me?

No, that's probably quite normal. Rebecca is also younger than I (—but why does she keep talking about everything as something that once *was*?).

I squeeze her hand. "I'll be there tomorrow, Rebecca," I say. "I promise!" Then I walk on through the house, maybe on my way out, I don't know, maybe to find other rooms and other faces that I haven't seen yet and that I must necessarily meet and see sooner or later.

The people who are there with Rebecca all turn their heads and look after me as I leave.

I walk through several completely empty rooms and stop at the door to a terrace. My back is suddenly like ice, now again, but this time it's because I know who it is I see: A tall, fat, bald man with a hatchet face and a crooked neck. Sheila pointed him out to me the other day from her window when we stood looking up toward the house here. All she said was: That's Marcel Chauvelot, the war criminal. There he goes up there in his hell. No one wants to have anything to do with him—except for those few who seem to be of the same ilk.

They are here, too: Kellermann with his one arm, the other one lost in the war, nobody knows how, is sitting next to him. I know him from the café. And out on an iron bridge leading from the terrace straight across the street to a dark garden stands Richard, whose scarred, white face is so horrifying that he goes out only at night. He is talking to another person, younger, almost a boy, on crutches. When everyone turns his face toward me for a moment, I notice that the boy is also blind and that a group of swarthy men are standing on the other side of the bridge smoking, where the dark garden starts. Men who could be from the town but who seem to be dressed differently. One of them motions to me, inviting me to join them and holding up a bottle that glistens yellow in the light. It's Manuel Pantorba, the restaurant owner from Santa Ana. And the other fellow—is he the one from the streets down there?—from the streets deep down there? or is *that* something I dreamed—breaks away from the others—just like down there—and comes over toward me. But I've already turned around and am fleeing—into the house, in through empty rooms and corridors, in through rooms with just one couple who let go of each other as I rush through or with chatting men who stop talking the moment they see me. My heart is pounding. I know that I'll never, *never* cross that bridge (—but what do I mean by that?)—that I'll *never cross* that narrow iron bridge *alive*, the bridge over to that remote garden to see what it harbors in the way of other figures standing there in the dark smoking and chatting and waiting for the future. (—What kind of thoughts is it that are trying to grab me, that are fishing for me tonight?).

And as I quickly walk away now, with long strides to hide the fact that I'm running—away from these figures, away from my own thoughts, if it were only possible—I suddenly remember…It's like a glaring projector catching me and holding me tight…I remember Sheila saying: "That's his house up there, the old mansion. They rent their apartments from him, only they don't know it."

Finally I find the stairs. Ready to drop I linger for a moment on the landing, leaning against the wall in a window niche. I can hear the others, the ones from earlier in the evening, whose names I know, making noise and talking on the other side of the wall, and now they are coming out here: Blond Pete and Rudy and Ted with Nora and

Diana and Katy and Louisa. Katy stands there for a moment, irresolute. She whispers to Louisa, and I hear the names Stan and Dick. But Louisa nods, and they walk on, to one of the apartments down below. Later Nicki and Annie come out, tightly clasped like the first ones, he grinning, she subtly sucking her front teeth; then Peter Holm and Walfriede, arguing wildly: they don't see me; then a strange procession of Maurice and Doreen, looking as if they were going to their own funeral, and of Cora who has latched on to the blue-shirted, blond painter with the wispy hair and the worn-down shoes and the pants with the drawings. I can't help smiling and thinking: I wonder if she'll bring it off? And Cora understands the little twitch around my mouth and winks at me behind his back.

Finally Ruth Sherman emerges. She stands for a second looking after them with her jumper in one hand and her patent leather bag clutched in the other. Her cheeks are red with anger.

"Those beasts!" she says out loud, stomping past me without seeing me, out into the courtyard with the crumbling lions, out into the night.

I look out the window. It's beginning to dawn. The native women come past, carrying baskets and white bundles on their heads. The bundles shine in the dim light. I feel so alone that I don't even dare think of it. If I did, I would go mad.

Suddenly I hear footsteps, and when I turn around, I stand perfectly still in the quiet hall, my heart throbbing in my throat. It's Henri, Henri Lourde, the hermit, who stands there smiling, looking at me. He has emerged from the interior of the house, but now he is already heading down the corridor out into the courtyard. I hear the gate banging down there before I decide to follow him, talk to him, I don't know why.

At that moment someone slips his arm under mine. I'm just about to fall when I see who it is, and I put my hands out before me so that it seems as if I'm clinging to him. It's Dave.

"Dave," I whisper, "is it you, is it really you?"

"Who else?" he says, pushing the lock away from his forehead. His eyes are a darker gray than I remembered.

"Sure, but where did you come from?" I ask breathlessly.

"From down there," he says nodding down the stairs. "I was a bit drunk this afternoon, you know. Then I found a cab, which brought me up here, I owed the driver money anyway. And then Nora invited me in to listen to music and have some more drinks, and I fell asleep, and then they finally came and woke me up."

I smile, but I feel my eyes getting misty. I tremble. For that reason I press closer to him. I have to fight down my desire to touch his face, straighten his hair to assure myself he is real.

"Where are we going, Dave?" I whisper.

"To your place. Where else!" he answers.

And we leave. For what else is there for me to do?

CHAPTER FIVE · *The Stranger*

Dave has just left. Someone over on the other side, by the parapet that a man supposedly was pushed off of the other day, is looking over toward my window again. A metal or glass object glistens in the sun, but I can't quite determine if it's a pair of binoculars. Even so, I'm loath to close the shutters against the fresh sea breeze, and it would be too hot if I just pulled the windows up. The window has been open most of the morning, until the sun hit our bed.

Now the figure disappeared over there—or went behind the shrubbery. I no longer see anyone.

I re-experience everything that has happened in this room since late last night.

I'm standing here again with Dave's arms around me, and he has kissed me. I'm dying to ask questions—about him, about me, about when and how we saw each other before? He is dying to remove my clothes and carry me over to the bed. I also know that we'll end up there, and maybe I even wish for it. Yes, a thousand times rather that than for him just to leave and for my questions to remain unanswered and for me to be alone again— alone. But something is keeping him from it.

"What is it, Dave," I say, stroking his hair. His features are handsome and striking, and it doesn't matter that it's weakness that has left such a deep mark on his face. I'm certain he can have all the women he wants.

He can have me, too. But I'm fighting a silent battle, which he mustn't notice, in order to gain my part of this trade with our unknown selves at this late hour of the night, this hour before it turns completely light and everything may become only too clear!

"You're so sweet," he mumbles, and I love being the woman he is saying this to tonight, love it so much that I have to bite my lip to keep from bursting into tears.

"There's something different about you tonight. The other times I had a hard time figuring you out."

My nails dig into his arms, and he holds me

tighter; but it's because I'm just about to give up, just about to scream or burst into tears or whatever, just about to cry out, "Dave, have we been together before? Answer me, for God's sake answer me!"

But there's no need to ask. I raise my head from his shoulder as if wondering (—as if a danger were past! and another not yet understood?), when I hear his voice again.

"You always said it would probably be best if we stopped seeing each other. After all, we saw most of each other when Anthony was gone. We sort of hid from him. You seemed to be afraid of him. But the last time, after he had left again, you said it would be best if we stopped seeing each other. You didn't want to let him down."

"And can I?" I mumble, pressing hard against Dave, for he has no idea what I mean, of course. It doesn't matter, doesn't matter at all that his hands begin groping under my sweater and unhooking the one hook that all women have on their bare backs.

"I don't know, but there's something so totally different about you tonight, Miriam," he says. "The last time you were so weird that I thought you were one of these people who take this stuff, you know. There are lots of them on this island, more than you might think. Did you, Miriam? Tell me honestly, did you ever?"

"No," I answer, "never! I never took anything like that!" And I hope I'm right.

"Just what is it about this Anthony?" he says. He pushes me away from him a little. He looks younger than ever, and there's a little yellow square like a tiny painted door in both of his gray eyes.—I try to swallow something I don't know what is, but there's nothing to swallow.

"Don't think about it," I say, helping him remove my sweater.

I cling to him as his hands caress me and slowly find their way down my back.

"Tell me, where was it we met the last time?" I whisper, holding his hands still for a moment.

"Why, don't you remember?" he laughs. "We were at the movies, and you got up and left when the show was just about over. It was one of these parting scenes you couldn't take. Your face was white as a sheet."

"And then we went for a walk?" I ask breathlessly.

He shakes me so that my bosom quivers. Has he begun to suspect something?

"What is it with you, Miriam? Don't tell me you've forgotten!"

"No, I guess it's just because I've tried to push that scene out of my mind," I say. "You saw yourself what it did to me. Tell me—tell me what we did next! Pretend it's a game we're playing so that I can make it up to you again if I let you down the last time."

"It was raining," he says. "It had been raining all day, but it was raining harder when we came out, and you put my scarf around your head…"

"Yes, yes, yes," I whisper triumphantly, "let me, it's my game, too…"

I cling to him, kissing him. A big smile quivers all over my body, which is almost naked now. A big smile, for I remember—almost. I can imagine how it must have been.

"Yes," I say, and I feel his hands doing with me what they will now, "…yes, and the streets were a mess, and we came back to this place. You sat here smoking three of your yellow cigarettes, and I tried to smoke one, too, but I didn't like it, remember? I've still got your cigarettes for you."

I'm breathless and relieved, and I suddenly don't know if it doesn't have something to do with the fact that I'm now completely naked and he is carrying me over to the bed.

"You're a sweetheart," he says, kissing my neck while kicking the bedding aside with his foot. A clever touch, a little trick, as if he had done it hundreds of times in his young life.

We lie together under the sheet. I know that my body will turn against me in a few seconds, that I will listen to and believe in its sweet, silent voices, that are like the voices of so many women, the voices of girlfriends, the voices of older women, and my own girlish voice from years ago, voices that all promise me joy and forgetfulness. I listen; they are all there! It's as if I'm in an invisible harem, and I've found my destiny: A man is with me now, and I'm going to be happy and feel his joy swell and penetrate me and bloom in the shortest of summers.

Total oblivion. Everything fades, is a blank. For a moment my mind is crystal clear and remote, far away from this man with his hot, restless hands which press against me. I could tear myself away now, get up, and get dressed. So why don't I?

Do not judge me, you other voice outside of this, the room of whispering women, outside of this warmth and sleep and fragrance with its unmistakable suggestion of strangeness and masculinity. I know it's you who makes my hand take hold of my neck as of a stone, now that something foreign is penetrating me. I know it's you that makes the sea roar louder down there with the voice of eternity, reminding me that I'm a stranger on this planet, in a strange room. But not now. Not the cliff over there and the streets and the fire and the figures. Not now…

I keep his hand away from the lamp as he reaches to turn it off. I don't want to forget this. I want to feel and remember these kisses that cover my face and sting my throat, even at the expense of never feeling and remembering anything else. I want to feel this force that extends me against my will, this column that I could kiss but that he hardly lets me touch. This hair which is like the forest on another coast, these eyes, which to me are wonderful, unfamiliar days that all the unceasing alertness and foaming readiness of my body are about to lead me into.

Easy now. I hold him tight, still. It doesn't last long. The lamp is still on, but another light glimmers behind the shutters. The walls disappear with the night. Yes, yes, yes, yes, yes, there's the sun, glistening and blinding and glistening…

"Darling," I say. "My love!" and I run my fingers through his hair, along his upper lip, which is covered with beads of perspiration. But suddenly I can't say his name.

Only after I've come back with his cigarettes and draped the sheet around me and am sitting there, looking down at his young, somewhat lanky body, which is not tanned like those of the others here but pale as ivory with hair so black it seems blue—only then can I say his name again.

"Dave," I say, "we had better get some sleep." I get up and hang a blanket in front of the shutters, so it's completely dark when we turn off the light a little later and go to sleep.

It's night again and sleep with long, sharp, wakeful glimpses, like at night when only the things closest to you are real, only the pillow, which is damp or wet with tears, only the wall with its peeling plaster, and the sea that is pounding behind the walls, and your own feeble warmth, the one that burns in your race, nobody knows from where.

And now, tonight—this breathing next to me, this other destiny resting here by my side, these members of another sex and of another name that fill my hands, indeed, that I hold on to as if I've lain down to rest on the slope of a cliff between rocks and roots, afraid of the sea down there, until I finally loosen my grip and sleep in spite of the dark. —Only to wake up, conscious of the fact that another person that I can't see now wants to still his fear here with me. I wrestle with him, silently, in the dark, until I finally vanquish him, this other person who seems to be created out of the cavities in my own body…and therefore is vanquished himself, does not open me, but is opened as I ride over him in my short victory, only to fall a little later, to sink, struck in a magic place, betrayed by my body, by the invisible women, who are all laughing now, while I fall, fall, forward, in toward that coast where everything is just warm darkness and emptiness now and tears that no one will see.

I'm tired now, and when I open the window, there's nothing other than the light streaming in from the empty, noisy room outside. In the kitchen a little later, I have to hold on to the counter as I stand out there on the tile floor wrapped in a towel, realizing that I forgot to push the box in front of the door out to the stairs and that I could have been caught in the act with this young fellow, who is still sleeping (—but why am I thinking these thoughts? Whom do I owe an explanation? After all, I wanted things the way they were. It was just that for one night, for one morning I didn't want to be alone—or was I?).

I fix breakfast and bring him his cigarettes. It's a good feeling to sit at the foot of the bed and talk.

"Know what, Dave?" I say, "I saw a really great caricature of you the other day. (Why am I using the term caricature? Why not sketch?). It was in Federico's portfolio, and I think Nickie made it.

But when I wanted to buy it, he didn't have it."

The smile that appears now, lighting the tiny, yellow doors in his eyes, that's what I've been waiting for, because it means that all I have to do is go over and get the roll, that he bought it for me just yesterday, and that it's in the inside pocket of his jacket. I already noticed it was there, but this way I can sneak the jacket with me behind the door while I unwrap the sketch and check to see if he has a key like mine or the same kind of large, new bills as the ones that were lying on my table the other day.

He doesn't.

"It's great, thanks a lot, Dave." I kiss him on the forehead, and he wants to pull me down toward him again. But I tear myself away, and when we sit in the bed again as before, he says:

"I asked Federico to hang on to it for me until I had the money!"

Isn't everything perfectly clear then? What am I worried about? Why am I trying to find dangers even where they don't exist? Why do I say to him now: "You're sure you didn't leave some money here at my place the other night?" only to get that smile and that answer I'm waiting and hoping for:

"If that were the case, you can bet I would have reminded you. I've been flat broke all week!"

"Was that why you kept avoiding me?" I ask, instantly flushed with fear of having said too much. But he smiles in his boyish way and lights a fresh, yellow cigarette. Then he throws the match on the floor and says:

"No, not really. That's the way you wanted it, you know."

"But you didn't avoid Sheila. I saw you down by the harbor." I'm suddenly furious at him, and I'm mad at myself for being mad at him.

But he is used to jealous women. He takes it nicely, so nicely, that it makes me smile.

"Sheila is very kind," he says philosophically. "She likes to have people around, so a friend of mine, who is living up in one of the old mills, and I, decided to drop in on Sheila around dinnertime a couple of times."

"What is your friend's name now?" I say. The palms of my hands smart.

"Al," he says evasively. "Don't you remember him?"

"Where is Al now?" I ask, but at the same time I know or realize that Dave and Al were living together before. I even think I remember.—"And where are you staying now?" I stare at him, and his gaze meets mine, but then he looks down.

"Al has been sick since the day before yesterday, with pneumonia. He's over there at the clinic where you were." Dave clears his throat.—"I mean, he has rented the mill out, so I borrowed a room at Nora's. But does that really make any difference, Miriam? It doesn't mean a thing! You know that very well. None of them are like you. All I want is for us to be together soon again just like we were last night." He reaches for my hand, but I stay where I am.

There's nothing more to say. He keeps smoking and dropping ashes on the bed. Maybe he feels it instinctively, but I know that there won't be a next time. Maybe if I hadn't hung that blanket in front of the window? If that darkness hadn't been there! But now that next time has already been. The light is so harsh out there, and I bite my lip and turn my face away from him.

"Didn't they take a good picture of you recently?"

I ask while he is drying himself after his shower and getting dressed over by the window.

He has just reached down to lace his heavy shoes, but he stops in the process, looking at me in amazement.

"No," he says, "I've never had that kind of money. That's expensive, you know.—You must be thinking of Anthony," he says with a touch of anger in his voice. "That was a good shot of him in the window down there. They removed it the day he left, I think. I was thinking all the time you had it!"

I can't very well ask him what Anthony looks like. For a second I stand there not knowing what to do, and he looks at me surprised and a bit hostile in spite of his weak features.

Then without a word I get my things together and take a shower. I hear him letting himself out and his steps disappearing down the stairs although the sound of my shower almost drowns out the sea down there, drowns out everything.

I decide to go up to Sheila's right away. Partly because she always asks why I don't come and have lunch with her. Partly to pass the time looking at her books and pictures so that I won't have to think for a while. Partly to see the entire house.

But I know very well that's not the whole reason, because it's also to find out, if possible, if she has got that picture of Anthony. And to see if Dave has been there—and if he has, what that might mean.

On my way up there I run into Federico, as always with the portfolio under his arm, in the company of the swarthy Egyptian fellow, Mustapha. They are on their way down together with Ingrid, the Swedish girl. When they have passed me, I notice that Federico has a leather strap across his shoulder behind the portfolio. But I can't see if it's attached to a camera or a pair of binoculars.

I also run into Nora just before I turn in at the gate leading to Sheila's house. She, too, is on her way down, and she smiles at me with her strange, amber eyes. I notice that she stops to watch me make my way past the dog and that she waves at me before moving on; then Maritza lets me in.

But Sheila seems hostile, cold. She simply mutters hello and leaves me to my own devices. I'm just about to take off again when she comes back a moment later and says: "Never mind me, Miriam. I've got one of my bad days, and besides, I have a headache. I've got to run an errand, but Maritza will fix you something to eat. Just make yourself at home until I get back."

I don't know how the news gets around this place, but it's obvious that she knows I've been with Dave.

Could Maritza...while we were asleep? But she doesn't have a key. Her smile is frivolous as always, when she brings the tray. It reveals nothing.

After lunch I walk around in the house. That was one of the reasons I came. There are light-colored tiles, plants, mirrors, birds everywhere, and in the large rooms there are rugs and weapons from many different places—and photographs. I'm just now walking through the long room with the globe and the huge blowups of the New York skyline and the other photos that seem so strangely familiar. I'm standing again at the desk in the niche. The drawers are locked. The bill from the camera shop that I saw last time has disappeared. As a matter of fact, it wasn't itemized either. The question is: Where is that photograph, that portrait of Anthony?

Now I'm on my way into that part of the house where I haven't been before—or don't remember having been. I look out the windows and count three patios—two small ones and one large one—with flowers and plants and more birds. On the large one there are tables in the shade, already set. It must be for the tea party this afternoon, but there are lamps on all the tables, as if Sheila is counting on the fact that the party will go on. I sit down on a small ottoman in a little gallery or corridor, from where you can look down into the square, tile-covered courtyard, where a jet of water is splashing out of the hand of a white cupid in a basin right between the columns and the tallest plants. No doubt about it, Sheila has got a beautiful place.

I notice that on the wall above the ottoman there's a contraption that looks like an old-fashioned radio.

The corridor widens and becomes a dark hall with a parquet floor, which is rare here on the island, and fragrant boxes made of camphor wood.

Where it ends, there's a white door with a Yale lock.

The door is locked…No, wait a minute, careful! It's supposed to be locked, but the lock has not caught right, and the door gives when I carefully depress the handle and give the white wood a little push.—It's as if I'm walking into a separate apartment. Again there's a little hall, a bath, a toilet, and a kind of kitchenette. Or is it a lab with gas burners and test tubes? There are some strange-looking glasses on the tiled table.

Isn't that a sound? I stand completely still, waiting, looking toward the door, which is standing ajar into the next room and beginning to move just a little…

But it's a cat, one more quiet cat, a large black, mangy cat making its way toward me without a sound. It rubs its head hard against my legs and eventually begins to purr, wanting to play.

But I'm too excited to bother about it. I push the door open and find myself in a dark, rather masculine room with leather furniture and with walls covered with dozens of photographs, some of them brown and quite faded, apparently old ones. A door stands open into another larger room. I stand perfectly still for a moment to ascertain if I'm alone. I try to muffle my heartbeats by pressing both hands against my chest. Then I open the Venetian blinds a fraction so that I can see the photographs on the walls.

I walk from picture to picture, and it's like walking in a bygone age. There are strange old trains and ships with sails and large wheels on the sides that look like the epaulets on uniforms. Most of all, there are pictures of women: a smiling woman with her hand on a grenade curtsying to a strong-looking man in a hunting costume; women in strange, long garments collecting the fare in old-fashioned buses; or women in straw hats and long, high-necked dresses riding on steamrollers out a tree-lined road.

There are other women in the same old-fashioned costumes and with their hair piled high, but with safety goggles on, working in a factory; and still others standing among so many grenades that it looks as if they are standing in a dairy filled with bottles.

There's an end wall with pictures as from another world, although the same things seem to be taking place there. But the costumes and the men's caps and beards are different, the houses are crowned with foreign-looking domes, and although the photographs are not in color and everything white in them has yellowed, there's an atmosphere in them as of blood and snow.

I walk over toward the door to the other room. On my way I see pictures of the same old buses, but with boarded-up windows now and full of uniforms as if they had gone far out of town or to another country to bring back their wounded soldiers. There's also a priest who is speaking from an old, square, flimsy plane. (When was the last time I saw a plane? I haven't heard or seen any while I've been here!)

There are many more pictures, and on each side of the door I'm standing in front of, two eerie photographs make a deep impression on me, maybe because I have a vague feeling of having seen them, or some that look like them, before.

One is of animals—is it monkeys? And where have I seen monkeys except for a little one that Sheila keeps down in the large bathroom? But didn't she talk about a bigger one, a dangerous one that she once had or still has? I can't help looking around. No one is there. I'm alone. I can hear Maritza moving about down below, scolding the two kitchen maids.

The animals are wearing bonnets or helmets with windows in them, and they are strapped into a kind of chair full of instruments. I don't quite understand what it is I see, but their flat snouts and eyes, which resemble the eyes of poor, old men, have a strangely moving effect on me.

The picture on the other side of the door is of beings dressed in bell-shaped helmets who are in the process of carrying coffins, apparently heavy coffins, because there are twelve to each coffin, on board a ship. I can't tell if they are human beings or animals, and I can't help shuddering. The ship's crew and a figure on the bridge seem to be wearing the same kind of helmet, which looks like a bubble. I shudder again and step into the next room. Here the furniture is daintier, lighter, and all the photographs are portraits. So maybe here!

First it is women, some with a vague, others with a definite resemblance to Sheila, as if she had appeared in all of these roles and fantastic costumes. Is she an actress? Hardly. They are more likely to be her family.

There is a hilarious, old, and slightly yellowed one, in which the woman who looks like Sheila has fur around her ankles and something that looks like a lamp shade on her head.

Again and again it is more or less the same figure in the pictures: the strong features, the slightly arched nose, the large eyes, which most likely are gray in real life, and the lush, prematurely graying hair—but the costumes change in a very funny way so that the wall gives the appearance of being a cabaret number with quick changes, as I walk along it. Now it is women in short skirts and with short hair, flanked by men with top hats in their hands and big bushy mustaches. Then it is cloche hats, low waists, and flowery dresses. Then there is suddenly a wealth of foxes over dresses of uneven length both in front and in back.

Here saluting Boy Scouts appear with bare knees—to be succeeded by strolling women in strange-looking pajama outfits, which turn into long skirts, short hair and spit curls again in the next scene. And all the time the same profiles, the same black eyes, the same features, the same family.

I wonder what they were wearing when I was born, whether I was carried under a trailing skirt with enormous bows, or whether I was warmed under giant foxes or fur capes, and whether my mother wore a tiny hat with an enormous ostrich plume when she checked in at the maternity ward.

My hands are shaking now, and I feel my nails hurting the palms of my hands again, but I quickly walk on, because now there is a long line of men in costumes that do not vary so much. All of them look straight ahead and kind of stare into the same mirror without getting an answer. I don't know any of them, not even at what point they begin to look like the men you see today. I examine every single face, but I don't know them, and they don't answer me. They just look right over my head so that I can't help turning around a couple of times.

Finally—after passing some pictures of men in uniform, some of them with strangely piercing eyes—I'm at the end of the line...But there, there something is wrong! A picture is missing, and the glass lies shattered on the floor.

I listen closely to the house and to myself. Again I hear the same shattering of glass I heard the other day when I was waiting for Sheila down in the long room with the globe…I listen and think.

Then there's another crash, but this time just behind me, and I whirl around…

It's Sheila who has banged the door behind her. I can see she's upset, but—she is also frightened! and—what is it now she is putting back in her purse and that glistens like metal?

"Sheila!" I call out. But the cry is stuck in my throat.

"And just what do you think you're doing in here?" she says in a hoarse voice, while her eyes look fixedly at me with a little quick movement from left to right, from right to left.

I walk toward her because I can't stand this even one more second. I'm ready to throw my arms around her neck, to tell her everything, to divulge my secret.—As it turns out, it's she who comes to my rescue. She kind of sighs and says:

"I guess I didn't shut the door right, and you couldn't know that I never let anyone in here.—

Well, now that you've seen my collection, are you satisfied?"

"Sheila," I whisper, "I didn't mean any harm."

"No," Sheila says, again with a sudden chill in her voice, "maybe you didn't mean any harm, but you *were* up to something. Don't you think I noticed you standing there, staring at the glass on the floor as if you were looking at a corpse…"

She stops short and makes a deprecating movement with her hand.

"Let's not talk about it, come along—down to the patio. Let's have something to drink. Did you have lunch?"

But I don't let her off easy. At this moment I'm the one who is strong and she is the one who is weak. I walk up to her and take both her hands in mine.

"What is it with you, Sheila? You had your gun out. What is it you're afraid of?"

"Forget it," she says, tired, "and may God have mercy if you ever…"

"But please answer me," I say. "Sheila, you are the only person I know on this island, and you must allow me to talk to you. If it was a picture of Anthony that was in that frame, then I'll understand.

We can still be friends."

Sheila looks at me for a long time, at first angrily, then surprised.

"It was not a picture of Anthony," she finally says. "What makes you think that?"

If I could only tell her why I thought that! Everything turns black before my eyes. I let go of Sheila's hands and slowly sink into a chair.

"Sheila," I whisper, "Sheila, for God's sake answer me! Do I know the person whose portrait you removed from the wall there?"

Sheila's eyes are suddenly grave. She stares at me for the longest time as if testing me. Then she says without ever moving her eyelids down over her pupils, which are suddenly large and black:

"I didn't remove that portrait. And I hope, indeed, I pray, if that's at all possible, that you don't know the person in the picture."

"But the other day," I say breathlessly, "wasn't it just the other day, when I was sitting down there...I mean, I heard the shattering of glass, I thought..."

"Yes, I heard it, too," Sheila says, "but Maritza is always so clumsy. When I discovered later on what had happened, I questioned her for a whole hour, but she swore up and down that she had neither heard nor seen anything. Afterward I suspected you, but you were there just a second later."

"Yes, I was down there," I say flatly. "But,—but weren't there other visitors that day. I mean, there was…"

"Yes, there was Clement, and Rebecca had been here. But that's impossible. I saw them out myself, and what would they be doing up here?" She falls silent, biting her lip and watching me again with black pupils and eyes that don't blink. I calmly meet her gaze, staring right back until she looks down.

"What's so important about that picture," I suddenly say angrily. "Why don't you just tell me who it was?"

But now it is Sheila who comes over and takes my hands and then strokes my hair. "Poor thing," she says, "ask me anything. But don't bring up that subject.—You're young," she continues with her voice close to my ear. "You have—or will have— so much that I don't have, not just the kind of life I no longer have but the kind of life I never did have. Let Sheila have her dark memories, the bygone years and all the people who are gone, all the people far away!—Let me have these rooms that are waiting for someone who never comes, these rooms that I must go in and out of and lock myself into just to understand that I've lived.—People are afraid to think of faces that no longer exist, faces they will never see again. But I look them up so that my mind shall not freeze, so that I may continue to feel warmth and cold, ice and fire and pain. Whenever you don't see me down in the town for a few days, it's because I've locked myself in here in the dusk of past years, of forgotten rooms, of my father's and grandfather's offices, to talk to women who are long since gone but who are still young here and to all these old faces, older than mine who smile and nod from these walls, making me think they are still alive. Now and then I believe them, and it's a wonder, but it's also one more sorrow, because then I also meet again with my opponents, whom I fear. They took my husband away from me and almost my mind as well. Why do you think I have all those mirrors in this house? And now, now that there's someone that I no longer know whether is dead or alive—if he is like us or if he is writing in pain inflicted by those who are out to get him…?"

The voice continues for a while, talking about other persons, other memories as if there is one…one thought in particular she is struggling with in order to push it down into the darkness, but I'm no longer listening. Sheila's voice doesn't stop until she notices I'm crying.

Rebecca has pulled me aside again. We have passed the tea around, greeted everyone, and talked about the weather. She drags me into the house and up the stairs, leaving the doors open behind us in her haste and eagerness.

"Hurry up," she whispers. "Come on, hurry! I want to show you something interesting."

Finally we get there. We sit down on the ottoman in the little gallery from where you can look down on the patio where the guests are gathered now like colorful birds in yet another of the aviaries of the house. In the meantime it has gotten quite windy, and the tree tops we can see from the window look like streams of smoke behind the roofs. But down on the patio it's idyllic and calm.

The guests are sitting at the little tables with the lamps, and while Rebecca busies herself with the old-fashioned radio with the headset on the wall above us, which I guess is what she wants to show me, I scan the tables.—There is Sheila with the Deansons, the older couple I saw in Santa Ana. Today, too, they are dressed in velvet from top to toe, he in brown, complete with cap and shoes in brown velvet, she—tall and thin as a rail and extremely talkative—still in pink velvet slacks, this time with a matching short jacket. I also notice the older man, Tom, with the crooked glasses and the two black canes at that table as well as the Swedish woman and her daughter.

At another table the Japanese are sitting by themselves, leafing through some old magazines they have found among Sheila's piles of newspapers and thrillers.

 Kellermann with the one arm is sharing a table with a tall, bald Dutchman with a bow tie; I think his name was van Zandt. They aren't talking. Kellermann looks as if he is bored and waiting for someone, maybe that sinister character who owns the apartments up in the old mansion and whom I saw him with last night. The Dutchman is carefully examining the plants that are growing next to the table.

Then there is a gentleman with a monocle who is being especially attentive to a slim, blonde, aging beauty with lots of jewelry, languid movements, and a long cigarette holder. They were introduced as William Vickers Adams and Juliette, which suggests they are a romantic couple (—like "Anthony and Miriam"; I tremble at the thought!). They are talking with Don Tomás, the lame priest with the big frizzy hair.

Then there are two Swedes whose names I don't remember. One of them, the one with the haggard face, is sitting in the sun with a straw hat on, black shoes, fringed pants, and a black leather briefcase, which he doesn't let go of. The other fellow is fair, with light, almost shiny blue eyes that can't quite see straight. I smile, for they have brought along their own rum, which they are pouring into the tea while looking around to see if anyone is watching.

They arrived in the company of the Swedish women.

Finally there's Rafael Vega with his long, powdered face. He is wearing an elegant, flat straw hat, white gloves, and a light-colored, plaid suit, and he sits there talking to a sickly looking man with a yellowish complexion, who is all dressed in black.

"Who is it now that is?" I ask, poking Rebecca and pointing. She sees the man I'm pointing to and says happily:

"Oh, that's Gregorio Navarro from the clinic; you know, the one who operated on your arm. As a matter of fact, they're the ones I'm listening in on."

Just now I notice that Rebecca has put the headphones on. Her long brown fingers are extended with eagerness, and her eye glistens. I stare at her in amazement: "You don't mean to tell me...Isn't that a radio?"

"No," Rebecca shakes her head. "Hush! There are microphones in the tables. Just listen." She hands me one of the headphones, and I hear Rafael Vega's voice and his fingers drumming on his straw hat: "What do you think about the situation, Don Gregorio? Will there be another crisis like the one we had a couple of months ago, when we all thought that was it? Or...?"

The other fellow clears his throat and says in a

low voice: "No, that's probably the worst it has ever been—aside from the actual outbreaks of war, which we have succeeded in controlling so far, at least in part. I don't think there will be any new crisis for a while, unless..." He pauses, and it's as if his gaze takes in the entire patio and maybe the surrounding town as well as it flits from table to table, past the window where I'm hiding, and comes to rest on Sheila for a moment—"...unless new evidence should appear in the matter that would render invalid the agreement already signed by the major powers, which, of course, places the responsibility on the head honcho himself and makes him a traitor, insofar as one can define that concept. I mean, it has always proved to be pretty difficult..."

"What in the world!" I cry out. "What is this?"

"I found out about it by sheer accident," Rebecca says proudly. "Isn't it a riot? Let's see now, how about trying another table, oh no, not that one..." She points to the table with William Vickers Adams, Don Tomás, and Juliette. "They are only talking about the weather. It's too bad, because sometimes they tease Don Tomás worse than anything. He has to live in celibacy, you know, and he is actually such a handsome fellow…Here, here is the table where Sheila is sitting. Just listen!"

Again she hands me half of the headset: "…that it was for sure that the man who plunged from the cliff the other day definitely was the victim of a crime." It's the Swedish "Mama's" voice, and I see the others nodding, except for Sheila who is sitting immobile. "…You see, they have learned—I heard this from someone living next to the victim, someone with a strange name that I don't recall—that his apartment was ransacked and that quite a few items disappeared. Someone seems to remember that he had a large collection of photographs—and some of them, I believe, were rather, eh, spicy, and those are all gone. They also say—yeah, isn't it terrible—that they found a piece of leather strap at the spot where he landed, which might belong to a camera. But the camera is gone. The murderer took it, swiped it, before he pushed him off. It was because of the strap they found out who the victim was. His face was totally unrecognizable."

"Mama is always so dramatic," Britta says, planting both elbows on the table, "but why is Mama referring to the murderer as a 'he'? Why must it necessarily be a man…"

"To be honest, I wouldn't put it past you." Mama's voice. "When it comes right down to it, there's not a thing you haven't been involved in on this island and not the creeps you haven't been seen hanging around with!"

All excited, Rebecca winks at me: "Isn't this something!" she says. "They always argue, and sometimes they even fight."

"Mama shouldn't have said that!" The large, strangely baby-like daughter with the sulphur-yellow hair and the square lion's face has jumped up, her fat cheeks beet-red. She pushes the table so that the microphone screeches. "Don't I take care of Mama and don't I go with her wherever she goes…?"

Rebecca can barely contain herself.

"Come on and sit down now, Britta!" It's Marilyn, the thin girl, who speaks up. Contrary to her usual practice, she has not gotten a word in edgewise for the longest time. "We've got to think of the motive. Come now, calm down, Mama, why would Britta…"

"Indeed, it's precisely the motive I'm thinking

of," says another voice, which I guess must belong to the fellow with the canes, because now he picks them up and balances them across his knees as if weighing his words. "Let's suppose for a moment that it was a camera he had with him, what would there be to take pictures of over there? The garden and the courtyard belong to a public institution where you usually see priests like our friend over there…" He nods in the direction of Don Tomás who is lighting Juliette's lilac cigarette. "…There's nothing to see on the beach. The only thing of interest is the large house over on the other side where I myself used to occupy the top floor. There's only one person living in the whole house now, the blonde girl who served the tea for us together with Rebecca. And by the way, I don't understand how she can be permitted to stay over there, because as far as I know the house is supposed to be renovated, and they have already had workmen in where I used to live.—That's why I moved, and now I've found a better apartment, thanks to our most gracious hostess here!"

Sheila laughs her hoarsest laugh but says nothing. Worried she looks up toward the drifting clouds as if she has thought of nothing the whole time other than the wind, which has now turned into a storm. As if she were expecting someone coming across the sea, or…

"But her windows are much too far away, of course, to be the subject of a photograph," the speaker continues, adjusting his glasses so that they are now placed crookedly in the opposite direction.

"Isn't there another girl who has a covered terrace out toward the sea there in the bay?" Albert Deanson asks.

"Sure," the cripple answers. "That's true. But you can't see it from there."

I have to hold the headphone away. The laughter hurts my ear. But a moment later Rebecca gestures wildly at me, whispering: "Hurry up and put it on again. Now they're talking about you!"

"…very pretty, but kind of quiet," Marilyn says. "I think her friend has gone away. You always see her alone now. I bet she misses him a lot. He was a good-looking guy, kind of an Italian type. It's my guess his name was really Antonio, even though they all called him Tony."

"Did he live in the apartment, too?" Mama asks caustically.

"No," the cripple says. "He stayed at a small hotel down by the harbor. I think he was a businessman and had something or other to do with the ships once in a while. I talked to him several times. He spoke all kinds of languages."

"It was touching how he took care of her during that first period when she had a broken arm and all and was lying over there in the clinic. I think she had been there for quite some time when we first heard about her."

"Yeah, it's strange no one saw her arrive," Deanson says now. "It's been almost two months since we first heard about her."

"Yeah, and Sheila has been great," Marilyn joins in. "Do you know anything about her situation or her family, Sheila?"

"No," Sheila says, "not a thing." She looks pensive, and the conversation apparently does not suit her. Her eyes are still following the drifting clouds up there.

I sit completely still, and I know I'm pale. I have

put down the headphone. Rebecca has tired of the game, too, and is looking expectantly at me, as if she were waiting for praise. So I'll probably disappoint her now.

"Just what does all this mean, Rebecca?" I say quietly. "Why are there microphones in the tables, and why are you showing me this?"

"Gee, I think it's fun," she says with her most dazzling smile, which pales little by little when she realizes I don't share her enthusiasm.

"Why does Sheila have all this paraphernalia?"

"I have no idea," Rebecca says, looking flustered. She smooths her checkered dress. "I discovered it quite by accident. Know what I think? I think it's some old junk she has inherited—she's got so much furniture and stuff, you know, and then she has installed it just for fun for a party or something…or," Rebecca brightens again, "maybe she is thinking of writing a book, a thriller. You know, the kind she always reads. She says thrillers have an 'entire' universe in contrast to most other books, whatever that means."

"Who would she have inherited that set from?"

"Why, don't you know…"—now Rebecca is beaming—"…that her grandfather was a famous detective at the time of Conan Doyle, and her father, well, he held a top position in the Central Intelligence of the Allies during the war…"

"And Sheila herself," I interrupt sharply, "where was she during the last war?"

"Yeah, you've got something there," Rebecca babbles. "She has never said anything about that." She purses her lips, thinking hard, but suddenly she looks out the window.

"Let's get out of here," she whispers. "Sheila has gotten up. Maybe she'll come up here. Come on, let's run down to the bathroom so she won't see us."

We dutifully wash our hands.

"Tell me something, Rebecca, are you in the habit of falling in love?"

She blushes. "Yes, much too often. I'm pretty sure I'm in love all the time, or if not, it's awfully hard for me to figure out whether I am or not."

"Who are you in love with right now?" I ask. "Surely not with Rafael Vega?"

"No, he's just such an attentive person," Rebecca says. "Let me see now, at the moment I think it's Don Tomás I'm in love with."

She turns beet-red all the way down her throat.

"Were you ever in love with Anthony?" I ask jovially, nudging her side.

Her color becomes like glowing iron.

"God, yes," she stutters. "You'll have to forgive me, Miriam, but, yes, I was." She is truly unhappy.

"Don't let that bother you," I say, struggling with my voice. "It must be hard not to. Do you collect pictures of the guys you fall in love with, I mean, the way some people collect photographs of film stars?"

Her yes is barely audible.

"Rebecca," I put an arm around her thin shoulders, while running my fingers through her thick hair, "Rebecca, would you happen to have a picture of Anthony? You see, I lost mine. I dropped it into the sea."—She doesn't know how true that is.

"No, Miriam, I don't, and if I did, I would run right home and get it for you." Both of her strangely clear eyes look right at me, and she squeezes my hand.

"Would you know of anyone who has got one?"

She thinks for a moment and then shakes her head.

"Rebecca," I say, "if you should ever come across a picture of Anthony, then try to get it for me one way or another, no matter how. And don't tell anyone I asked you."

"No, Miriam, I promise…but where are you going? Don't you want to go down to the others again?"

"No, dear," I say, kissing her on the cheek while tying a scarf around my head because of the wind, "I feel kind of tired. Give my regards to Sheila and tell her thanks for everything."

I don't know where I'm going. I simply keep walking. I feel like a chessman among other pieces which are constantly threatening me with unpredictable moves, but which are camouflaged so that I can't see which ones can hit me from afar and which ones threaten me from the next corner or the next gate. I walk across the square by the harbor, and there I see Tubby and Peter Holm and Walfriede—I can hear the excited voices of the couple from far away—sitting together with Blond Pete, all ready for his trip with his suitcases next to him. Most of the girls are there, too. But *who* are Tubby and Peter Holm and Walfriede and Blond Pete and Katy and Louisa and Diana and Ingrid and Doreen? Who is this Federico who is on his way over to their table together with Mustapha and who is struggling with his portfolio as if it were a sail? I walk along the square with the monument, past the green kiosk underneath the trees. Outside of the yellow bar are Rudy and Ted and the painter in the blue sweater and the Browns, the married couple, trying to keep the tablecloths from flying away in the storm, which has already broken large branches off the trees in the square. I wonder why they don't move inside or remove the tablecloths, and I also wonder who Rudy and Ted and the painter and the Browns are—and Dick and Stan, who are sitting inside the kiosk, as I see now, and the photographer who is standing behind his glass door over there—who they all are.

As I walk toward the middle of the square to avoid the falling branches, I suddenly see the Swede with the haggard face and the black briefcase, the one I just saw on the patio up at Sheila's, standing near the camera shop staring after me, the black briefcase still under his arm. When I turn around a little later on my way out of town, he has vanished.

Out in the hills with the olive trees I see Nora and Cora—crazy names!—walking arm in arm on a path down below. The storm must have made them hurry back from the beach. Cora is wearing her usual costume (I think she has got only the same one), but Nora has some incredibly short shorts on that make her well-shaped legs appear unusually long and cause one not to notice how large she is around the middle. They wave hard at me when they see me, but I don't feel like talking, so I just wave back and keep on walking. I notice that Nora walks with a slight sway as if she might have hurt her hip at one time. There's suddenly something clown-like about both of them, which makes me stop again to look after them. I can see from where I'm standing up here that Nora has put a pebble in the depression of her sun hat to keep the wind from blowing it off, and I smile at the thought of what would happen if she should forget and reach down to pet a dog.

I pass the bladeless windmill, which must have been Al's and Dave's, and I notice a heavy figure with a brutal profile next to it. It's Marcel Chauvelot, the owner of the "mansion" up above, who is standing there looking out over the sea. Is he the one who has taken over the mill? Or is he just out for a walk? I don't see Dave anywhere.

I choose another path, and I walk for a long time. Finally I'm back in town again, standing outside the theater. It's got another marquee today. The early showing is just about to start. I go in.

I'm dead tired, and it's not until later that I realize it's a submarine movie I'm watching. I don't know how long I've been sitting there in the dark with the flickering beams of light above my head, thinking all the time it was the dreams of my own tired brain I was watching.

An anchor with a line is being lowered into the foaming water, and high above lies the surface of the sea like an enormous, glittering precious stone of a wonderful bluish-green color.

Then there are figures, dressed in fantastic outfits and with long pearly streaks of air trailing them, who tumble backward down through the water. Suddenly they all turn around and quickly head for the deep. I see their long legs with flippers on waving up from the dark before they disappear altogether.

One of them returns, staring at me for the longest time out of his mask, which has only one large, oval eye, behind which I can just make out the features of a human being.

Suddenly a light-colored object is swimming around in the emerald water, which is now all around, above and below me. Even up above it's getting dark now. I'm way down there, and I know I must go even deeper. I follow the flippers, which motion for me to follow them to the deep. But I shudder, hesitating for the longest time paralyzed with fear, when I realize that the light-colored object is a lifeboat with its air chambers smashed on the one side, floating around in the void. A white hand clutches the railing from inside the boat, but I close my eyes. I don't want to see who it is; if I do, I know I'll call out a name—and not be able to…

When I open my eyes again, I'm even deeper down. It must be the figure with the flippers, still motioning in front of me, who has led me down where it's dark but from where lots of pearly streaks rise as if a multitude were already on their way down below. At that moment I discover I'm holding a line in my hand, and in that same instant I realize, again, that I'm just watching a movie...

But it's not until a few seconds later, when my back turns to ice and I hear myself uttering a stifled scream, that I feel I've still got the line in my hand. I pull my hand away with yet another cry and notice I've grabbed hold of the thin leather handle on the shabby briefcase belonging to the Swede, who is sitting next to me.

I feel all the faces in the theater turning to look at me, and I see him staring at me with his pale, haggard face, which the beams of light above our heads flickers across, so that it looks as if he were telling me something in extreme haste although he is actually sitting completely still. Mumbling an excuse, he gets up a little later and sits down a few seats away.

I want to leave, but I'm too weak. I should never have gone in here alone. I don't have the strength

to get up, so I stay where I am with pounding heart
and aching hands, watching how the frogmen with
their fins and these heads that are like bubbles
make their way with difficulty to the sunken ship,
which is completely covered with moss like a rock;
but how they then swim inside it, how the ma-
hogany still glows red, and the brass gleams yellow, and everything is intact, complete, in perfect
condition, as one imagines the dead might live, only
outside of the world and without meaning. Everything happens here in this never-ending silence
where what we used and owned yesterday is now
being forced toward the panes, floating around our
heads in the shape of chairs and tables and mat-
tresses—and there, there like a mass, whose face I
can't see; floating there like words that have been
detached from their meaning, way in there in the
silence and now slowly revolving around themselves, pushing us in their madness; this madness
that continues in the form of schools of striped fish
with funny faces swimming through the salons, and
the dark fish of prey lying in wait in the lifeboat on
the sloping deck, and these masked beings who are
now as in a grotesque dance pointing to their in-

struments and numbers, swaying as if they were drunk and pointing again and again to something that looks like enormous wristwatches, as if they were looking for an age and a time that no longer exist.

When I come out, I hear the steamer hooting. Taking back streets, I hurry down toward the harbor, and when I turn a corner I notice that the Swede with the briefcase and the ridiculous straw hat is walking in the same direction.

The ship is just now turning around. It is immense, taller than the houses along the waterfront. It looks like a glistening, illuminated city that is slowly coming closer and closer.

I sit down out by the outermost bar where I saw Sheila that day with Dave. I can see that men are standing ready with hawsers and that the ship is docking there. The Swede finds a table farther down the quay at the next café. He has already had his glass filled twice, and he is glancing in my direction, but then he looks out toward the ship and lights a cigarette.

After a while Nora arrives. She sits down at my table, babbling about this, that, and the other, and then offers me something to drink.

I gratefully accept what she orders for me, but I barely hear what she's saying. My eyes are glued to the ship, which is now just a few feet away from the quay. I can see a dozen figures and faces at the railing in the light of the powerful floodlights that have just been turned on. But no "Italian type" that could possibly be "my Anthony."

"How about another drink?" I say to Nora. "It's on me."

Chuckling, she stretches out her long legs— which are never quite close together—in front of her with her toes turned in.

"Sure," she says delighted, "but then you'll have to help me find a cab afterward. I'm zonked!"

We drink in silence while I look around and Nora examines her toes.—Deanson is also down here, and isn't that Sheila way over there? But now she's leaving again, disappearing into one of the streets.

Blond Pete is standing ready with his suitcases, and the whole gang is gathered around him. In front of them are Rafael Vega with William and Juliette. Every time I look over at them, one of them is lighting Juliette's cigarette. The wind has subsided, so you would think it wouldn't be so difficult.

Mustapha and Federico and the Swedish girl, Ingrid, who never says anything unless she is asked and doesn't even smoke like the others, comes over and sits down behind Nora and me, and we turn around and nod to them. The sick doctor nudges Rafael Vega, behind whose chair a man in uniform has been standing for a long time. A policeman? I've actually only seen them at the entrance to the bank. Or is it the tall, gray man with the cap and the book? I can't tell.

Now the gangway is lowered, and people begin to disembark. I suddenly notice that the invalid with the crooked glasses and the two canes is standing all the way over by the ship together with the boy with the flaxen hair, whom I haven't seen since "my first evening."

Most of the passengers have come ashore now. They have been received and embraced by the native women or have started out at a brisk pace. And here comes a big fellow, dressed in a velvet jacket and with a paint box over his shoulder and an easel in his hand like an old-fashioned artist. He has a large red beard which glistens in the light cast by the floodlights. Have I seen that face before? No, I don't know any men at all with red hair—except for Tubby—(but what and whom do I know anyway?). There's something vaguely familiar about his face, which I can't quite make out because it's in the shadows now. The painter looks around. He is obviously a stranger to this island.

Now the boy with the flaxen hair says something to him and picks up his suitcase, and they walk over to a little hotel on the promenade behind the terrace where Rafael Vega is sitting. I see him popping up in a window on the second floor and opening it. The boy doesn't come out again. Apparently he is employed at the hotel, which looks extremely modest.

"That wouldn't be the hotel where Anthony used to stay?" I say to Nora. She is talking to Rebecca, who has joined the group behind us in the meantime.

She laughs with her tongue sticking out between her teeth.

"You've got some memory," she chuckles. "No, it was over there." She nods in the direction of a larger house farther down the promenade. "And I don't think we'd better have any more to drink," she says with that other smile of hers, which makes her thick-lipped mouth quite small. "Don't forget you promised to find me a cab. Don't you want to come on up?"

I shake my head no. I simply don't have the strength.

When she and Rebecca have left, chattering and giggling like two schoolgirls, and the cafés and chairs along the promenade are almost empty, something happens that surprises me a little: Maritza suddenly arrives, elegantly dressed, and sits down where Rafael Vega was sitting. She powders her nose, paints her lips, orders coffee, and sends the waiter into the hotel with an envelope, which she removes from her purse. A little later I see the bearded painter pull the curtain aside and look out.

Maritza waits for a while, then she pays, and walks over toward the ship, where she strikes up a conversation with a couple of the officers standing at the gangway. Then she goes onboard the ship and accompanies one of them to his cabin.

Presumably it is her way of earning extra income.

I must have slept for several hours, when I wake up realizing that somebody is in the apartment.

The sea is still thundering down below after the storm, but I distinctly hear footsteps and a door creaking. In that instant I know I forgot to push the box in front of the door, because I was so exhausted when I came home that I simply plopped down on the bed with my clothes on and fell asleep.

I can't take any more of this. I don't dare cry, but everything within me is an endless weeping that freezes up with fear. In my despair I wonder just how many times a human being can die…(—and I don't know why that thought keeps returning, mocking me.)

I'm paralyzed with fear. Without even being aware of it, I have folded my hands, and they will no longer let go of each other. I slip down on the floor and lie there on my knees, in a heap, really, without thought and without words with my clasped hands on the bed. Dully, someplace way in there in the back of my consciousness, something in me thinks that it's as if my body wants to come to my rescue at this terrible moment, by folding me into the position of prayer when I myself am not able.

I hear the steps coming closer and the door creaking into the room on the sea where I'm lying. I'm pretty sure it's a man. Now the stranger is in the room, standing behind me, but just for a moment. Before I have time to scream and prepare for death, before I have time to turn around—I'm curiously weak; I *can't* move—the door creaks again, and I hear the footsteps retreating and the front door banging.

A long time afterward, an eternity afterward, I turn around—slowly like the ship that turned in the harbor—and grope my way toward the light switch.

Again a wad of bills is lying on the table, cigarette ashes are strewn on the floor, and I notice scratches of hobnailed heels on the tiles.

CHAPTER SIX · *Meetings*

The fear I experienced last night, when I thought everything was over, has been like a shot in the arm. I haven't slept since, but I've taken a bath, and I feel calm and collected. Now the battle has begun.

When Maritza arrives (It's her day; but why does she come here in the first place? You'd think there would be plenty for her to do at Sheila's house. Did Anthony and Sheila…?)—when she knocks at the door and I hear her voice, I'm in the middle of examining the blurry newspaper picture on the front page of the paper she brought me the first time I "saw" her. The more I look at it, the more distinct do the features of the red-haired painter who arrived last night become, and I'm more and more convinced that it's the same person. In addition, I still have this vague feeling of having seen that face before, even though I don't remember anything concrete about it, of course, any more than I remember anything else.

I can't talk to Maritza, but I point to the paper, letting her know through signs and gestures that I'm surprised she doesn't bring newspapers with her more often.

She starts talking a mile a minute, and little by little I realize she had brought it along that day by mistake and that she had been thoroughly reprimanded by Miss Sheila, who as a result was forced to run all over town trying to locate another copy of that same paper.

(Why didn't she come to me for it?)

Maritza starts cleaning the apartment while I examine the blurry picture for the umpteenth time, scanning this text which makes no sense to me. Only now do I notice a very short article in bold print, which is continued on another page. I finally find it and recognize a word here and there like "Rusia" and "nuclear" but no name that would go with the portrait except maybe the italicized word "El Colonel," which must mean the same as the corresponding English word, colonel.

I fold the paper. I even go so far as to toss it in under the stove, which is turning red from rust because of the sea air. Then I give Maritza my most radiant smile, as radiant as I can make it today, and—again with gestures and signs—start complimenting her on the pretty outfit she was wearing the night before. Her eyes sparkle, and I get bolder, drawing her a ship in the air and hooting like a steamer, whereupon I put my head on its side as if I were sleeping and eventually embracing an invisible person.

She laughs and nods eagerly, and I laugh with her. I hope she doesn't notice I'm perspiring from all this effort. I assume she knows all about my relationship with Dave (—and Anthony! something screeches inside of me so that I'm about to step out of my role and have to hold on to the table), and this puts us on an even footing. And now comes the culmination, the climax to our merriment, because now I laugh in a way so ugly that I had no idea I was capable of anything like that, miming a beard on myself, waddling uphill like a man loaded down with a paint box and an easel, up to Sheila's—I point in that direction, whispering her name, whereupon I double up with laughter (it's not hard), slapping my thighs and making sleep- and love pantomimes and dancing around the kitchen, while Maritza stands there holding on to the door and is about to die of laughter. When it subsides, she gives me a significant glance, nodding and pointing: Oh yes, he is up there all right! whereupon she has a new fit of laughter, but she eventually collects herself, putting a finger to her lips and crossing herself a couple of times, indicating to me that this is a secret and that she never said a thing.

I wait in the shadows of some shrubs below Sheila's house. On the way up there I run into the eccentric Swede, who is without his black briefcase today. He is wearing a different outfit, and he seems to be more sober. At first he wanted to avoid me when he saw me, but when that was impossible without seeming obvious, he tried to smile at me. He didn't quite succeed.

He was wearing wide, black shoes that looked as if they might have hobnailed heels.

People look suspiciously at me as they walk past, but I pretend something is wrong with my sandal, all the while keeping an eye on Sheila's house.

When I look up toward the row of houses higher

up, I seem to see someone standing there again watching Sheila's house through a pair of binoculars. The figure is standing in a window right above the white-plastered basement floor of the "mansion." It would appear to be a man, and the figure is too husky to be Dave's. Is it Marcel Chauvelot?

I don't want to be seen either by him or by Sheila or by the dog, so when the red-bearded painter comes out, I wait for a long time before I start to follow him. I can see his hair shining between the shrubs up above, while I make an effort to catch up with him so I can see where he is going. When we get up near the mansion, I take another street just to play it safe, and for a moment I think I've lost him and that maybe that's where he has gone in, but then I suddenly see him right out in the sunlight again in the next street. He is walking slowly, looking up and down the facades of the houses as if he wants to draw them or paint them, but he finally stops, looks down the street but without noticing me standing in the shadows, and walks in through a gate.

My heart beats so that I have to press my fists against it, and it has time to beat hundreds of times before I myself step in through that same gate.

It is cool in the entrance hall, and it echoes in there as in a church. I'm surprised at my own courage, but I've noticed he is wearing bast shoes, and I simply *must* meet this man whose figure (and again a flash of fear shoots through me. His figure?)—whose stature and walk seem even more familiar than his face.

I hear voices in the distance coming from the reverberating, vaulted room, and I sneak closer between the white, plastered walls, up some low steps. These turn into a broad landing, which goes around a corner and ends at a bolted, white-painted gate and which gets its light from some large windows with green curtains across the lower part. The windows are encased in a paneled wall facing some sort of office whose door is ajar. I can't see any other doors or exits except for a little low door farther down, presumably leading to the basement, and a gallery high above running straight across the stairwell with a door at each end.

I sit down on a stone bench across from the glass wall, behind which I can still hear voices, two voices. It's two men's voices, and very little time has passed before I realize that I recognize one of these voices. It's that of Clement Gallus. I know it although I can't see him. I can see only his shoulders and his elbow when he moves in his chair.

I can't see the other person with the deeper and somewhat older voice, but it might well be the burly painter I followed, who is sitting across from him and whose shadow becomes visible through the green curtain once in a while when he leans back in his chair.

I feel safe knowing that Gallus is near, and I calmly survey the part of the study that is visible through the crack in the door. On his desk is a heavy paperweight in the shape of a crystal, which catches the light from another window facing a patio. The furniture is of a reddish wood, and the back wall is filled with leather-bound volumes, whose smell wafts out through the doorway together with the smoke from a cigar. (I know this smell of books and cigars; it almost makes me cry!). Maybe that's why I don't knock and make my presence known but merely remain seated, waiting.

Actually a little tyrannical kitten prevents me

from doing that. I've been watching it prancing back and forth on the desk, trying to swipe at the pattern of light from the large glass crystal. Now it has jumped down on the floor and is darting in and out the door, rubbing itself against my ankle and running back again. It is probably because of it that the door is ajar. It is clearly an offspring of Sheila's large cat.

It has been quiet for a while, and I've heard the sound of matches and the clinking of glasses. It is resonant here as in a church or a grotto, and I can't help overhearing everything that's being said.

"You always talk about 'the mistake,'" says the other calm, deep voice, "but let's assume for a moment that it isn't a mistake but that everything simply happened the way it had to happen!"

The green glow from the curtains and from the plants and shrubs behind the other window causes the little part of the study that is visible through the door to be bathed in an unreal light. It is as if a conversation were being resumed after many years have passed. After an entire lifetime! I think. It is also as if there's a third person present in there, one who is just listening in. But maybe that's just my imagination. Maybe I myself am that third person who is listening now.

"But you'll have to admit," Clement Gallus says, "that it's monstrosities that are taking place. I don't want to dwell on the interrogations and the persecutions or the arms that are being sanctioned. You need only think of the dilapidated sepulchral church in Jerusalem where Syrian, Greek, Roman, Armenian, Coptic, and Abyssinian priests perform their blasphemous rites, each one between his crosses on the wall and within his chalk lines, which they have fought over and negotiated for themselves."

"There are worse blasphemies," says the calm voice. "Only good things are being done in the name of the Church, even though its servants are weak and all abuses are temptations that have been resisted. I think history has proved that."

"That isn't true of the weapons, and incidentally you always say that!" There's despair in Gallus's voice now. "And it's precisely this certainty of yours that makes me afraid—afraid of making another mistake, indeed afraid of having made a mistake. Because even though I belong to a brotherhood, as you well know, I *did* after all leave this incense-smelling mother church, this foreign temple where it's as if the incense drifting under its vaulting comes from the old tribal spirit whose language was fire and brimstone and whom a people gone astray under the heavens pronounced its god.—I've never ceased to wonder at man's patience when I think that for two thousand years now we have been studying and spelling our way through these accounts of a distant land and a culture that we don't know the least thing about and hardly have any possibility of understanding—and at how we can accept this institution which with its thousands of black figures personifies this all-seeing, all-hearing divinity by being omnipresent around us, so that even those who break away, compelled by something inside themselves, must always dwell in the shadows of this church."

"There is a reason," says the deep voice now, falling silent for a moment as if creating its own silence. It's already clear that it can hardly be the painter who is doing the talking. Maybe he is the third person whose presence I'm feeling. Or he has gone into some other part of the house and will probably be back. So I stay where I am. The cat is up on the desk again playing with the rays from the prism, which constantly change according to the movement of the leaves in the wind on the patio. There is no other sound out there than the wind in the shrubs and the trees.—And now I hear the calm voice again while the cat chases like mad after the flickering pattern of light on the desk:

"You see, the reason is that this cult is the order of life, the way most people live it and which all of us are born into. You have a father, a mother, and a son, and the priests have castrated themselves symbolically to serve this mother of God who was favored by the Almighty. Isn't that clear as can be?"

Gallus's voice is hoarse with emotion: "Yes, but a cult can also die. Its time can be over, and I've seen it die in a lot of places. You know just as well as I that it does happen. It's a question of faith whether you care to believe it still exists in its original form or not."

"Yes," says the calm voice. "I believe that. Otherwise I wouldn't be here."

"It's strange," says Gallus after a pause, during which the kitten has collapsed on the table, exhausted from its game, and is just lying there now, stretching and licking itself. "Think of those vast lower layers of society that have emerged. Think of this energy of theirs, this enthusiasm of theirs which ignores the Church. Where does this energy come from?—You know I've been tempted. Think of these young, determined footsteps that can be heard these days in the new cities and in the old ones which are quickly growing into a new age. Think of the visions that are motivating them, of Tokyo with over twenty million inhabitants in a few decades, becoming the metropolis of history, a system of planets of cities full of air and light and order—without temples."

"Things won't turn out the way you think," says the voice a bit tired. "There will always be temples in a city like that, lots of temples. Just think about it for a moment. You've seen it happen!" There's anger in his voice now. "Its name will be *legion*, and you have already seen the *wings of abomination* fill the air." It's the voice of a priest I'm listening to.

"Yes, but now things are different again," Gallus says. "Things are moving so fast."

"Yes, right into the lie," the other voice thunders. "I've been afraid of war like everyone else, and I've prayed to be released from this fear; but what I have instead at this point is a fear of peace, of the strange times that will come with the infinite crowds. Do you know what it is—these millions that multiply with millions, these empires that arise and grow out of these times, as if we were already no longer living on Earth but out among the stars in the void?"

"Tell me." It is quiet. There's only the wind outside and the pattern of light flickering silently across the table. The other voice is silent for a long time. Then I hear it again:

"No one has kept watch from the nave of the Church for centuries, but now the shore of the underworld is already in sight!"

"You have no right…no one has *any* right to say that." Gallus's voice is like a scream.

At that moment you can hear the scraping of a chair in there and a third voice muttering something. Then the door opens.

It's not the painter. It's Henri Lourde, looking at me surprised at first and then smiling.

"Was it…was it you who were talking just now?" I utter. I have lost all self-control.

He puts a finger to his lips. "No, it was the bishop," he says. "But why are you sitting here? Come along!"

We walk down into the entrance hall, and I explain that I followed a red-haired, red-bearded painter who arrived on the ship yesterday because I thought I knew him; that I saw him walking in through the gate and that I sat down on the bench to wait until he came back. While I'm telling him this, he looks at me attentively. His eyes, which have many colors and are light blue closest to the pupil, are alert and friendly. A tendon twitches in his throat above the open sport shirt, and lines of worry appear on his high forehead below the almost too curly dark-blond hair.

"Yes, he was here all right," he says. "But he went to the wrong place. He wanted to see Don Ramon, the old painter who lives next door, so we showed him the rear entrance. It's the little door there leading up to the gallery."

He drops the hand he is motioning with, hesitating a split second. Then he says: "Come on. Let's go up and see if he's still there."

I don't answer. I simply nod and follow him in through the low door, which we both have to stoop to get through, up the narrow dusty stairs while I keep wondering what to say to the painter. After all, I was counting on seeing him alone. When Henri knocks at the door up there, my brain has ceased to function. I stand there, staring at his large hobnailed shoes.

A stooped old man in a white smock and beret opens the door. He has a brush and palette in his hand.

"No, Michael…" he clears his throat, "I'm sorry that gentleman already left, but if the young lady would like to…"

Things go black before my eyes. Michael, *Michael,* MICHAEL…! something shouts inside me, a cacophony of voices strangled in gargling as if I were about to drown.—I want to shout, shout the name *Michael* with all the power in my lungs, but my mouth is full of water, and I'm about to suffocate…

Henri catches me, and when I come to again on a green chaise, the old man has put his brush and palette aside and is bending over me with a glass of water in his hand.

"It must be the stairs," he says, "or maybe the young lady ate something…" His old eyes smile at me between thousands of wrinkles above his half glasses while I sip some of the water.

I look around the studio, and it's as if I were dreaming in a land of pictures (—as if I…; no, *no!* —and I turn around, burying my face in the pillow they have put under my head…).

But later on I take a look around, and then it is more as if the pictures in this dim, quiet studio, where the old man is already working away again at his easel, are not something I am dreaming but are somehow pictures that are dreaming *me,* as I lie there in the middle of their space now, looking from one to the next.

They are like fairy tales I heard at one time and since forgot, fairy tales that I meet up with again now much later like riddles insisting on being solved by me.

I am somewhere way back in my forgotten childhood, but at the same time I have walked a long, long way and happen to be *here*—in this quiet house, where the old man is working away at his easel and looking up over his glasses at the female figure coming to life on the canvas, albeit infinitely slowly, still so incomplete, as if every single barely perceptible stroke of his brush is one hour or one day in the life of this figure, and each line, each clear outline must be figured in ages and years.

I can't make out all the pictures on the wall very clearly, but there is always a single figure on a road or a bridge, in a forest or on a mountain road. Somewhere a bush is burning by the roadside. Somewhere a crossroads raises its cross, and a figure is sitting at its foot.

The pictures are clear like the pictures in children's readers, books that I, too, must have owned at one time. Calmness issues from them to me, as if I am at a tension point in the very inside of their circle. I have no idea how long I lie there watching them before I realize that Henri Lourde is sitting silently in a corner looking at me.

It is dark where he is sitting, and I can't see his eyes. At first I am frightened, but then—to my own amazement—I get angry.

"Well, don't you ever say anything?" I almost

yell, so that the old painter's brush comes to rest and his eyes look at me over his glasses. "Do you always just sit there and say nothing?"

"There are many ways of speaking," he answers smiling. His answer irritates me at the moment just as his hair annoys me no end, because it's much too soft and wavy for his large, angular figure. I'm sure it was the main reason I passed out earlier.

"Once I start to talk, I might not stop," he says, smiling kindly as he comes over toward me. "And I'm not sure you'd like that." His face becomes serious again, almost sorrowful. The old painter keeps working away as if he doesn't hear our conversation.

"When can I see—Michael?" I stutter confused.

I seem to notice the two men exchanging a glance. Then Henri says: "He'll be back tonight at eleven. You're welcome to see him here."

"Isn't he at his hotel?" I snap.

"No," Henri says curtly. "He's not at his hotel.— Can I get you a cab so that you can get a little rest before tonight? Or do you want to stay here?" He doesn't offer to go with me.

"No, thanks," I say. "I've got to go. Thanks for everything."

As old Don Ramon opens the door for me, he says softly, and it is as if Henri is forcing him with his glance: "Michael...is a friend of my son's. I set great store by him, you know...eh, it would be best if you'd take care that no one follows you here to-night."

On my way down the hill toward town I get into a steep street where I haven't ever been before. It leads downward from a square with trees and a wall at the end, and I suddenly realize it must be from over there that you can see straight across the little bay to my windows. The lame priest, Don Tomás, just happens to be standing in front of the gate, adjusting his briefcase. I believe it's black.

I quickly walk down the steep street, but I can't walk too fast without slipping on the smooth pebbles. There is a red-painted tin cross at the corner that looks like the primitive figure of a human being with a square glass jar filled with flowers and an extinguished candle where the heart would be, and farther down also what looks like a lantern with white wax flowers behind the glass where the private parts would be. All the way down the street, large, red wooden crosses are spiked into the walls, and it's as if I were fleeing between these symbols of the color of blood, finding my way down through an invisible stream of people on their way up the hill, whereas I'm the only one who wants to go down. My nerves are frayed.

At the bottom of the street I stop because I hear the sound of children's voices coming from a school, and I suddenly see through a narrow peephole above a low parapet with medieval embrasures the path to Sheila's house lying just a stone's throw away and Sheila herself at the window.

Has she seen me? Is it a pair of binoculars she is getting out now? Can't be. I'm completely hidden from view. Or is it the revolver she is removing from her handbag for a moment, examining it and putting it back again?

Farther down I run into Rafael Vega who greets me in his exaggerated fashion again, turning around and looking after me, gloves and hat in hand, as I walk on.

When I'm almost all the way down by the square, I see at some distance Dave with Katy and Louisa, whose skin color appears absolutely marble white, almost violet in the afternoon sun. I take another street to avoid running into them, and it suddenly seems odd to me that Dave should happen to appear the other night at the very moment when I had decided to follow Henri Lourde.

When I hear running steps behind me a moment later and feel a hand on my shoulder, I figure it's Dave again and reluctantly turn around.

But it's Rebecca, and it takes a few seconds before she gets her wind back.

She looks so strangely at me. There's something frightened and surprised in her gaze. Then, after having looked around, she removes something from her beach bag and gives it to me.

"This is what I promised you," she mutters. "Hide it, I've got to run. I've got a date."

She is already gone when I feel my nails digging into my palms again.

I stand there staring at the photograph I'm holding in my hand, of a dark, husky, handsome man, who looks Italian. His chin and mouth are brutal, and his piercing, hypnotic eyes make me utter a little scream when I see them again.

On the picture it says in a handwriting that re-sembles printing: TO MY DARLING FROM "ANTHONY."

I start as I notice the invalid with his two canes and his crooked glasses standing there watching me from across the street.

CHAPTER SEVEN · *Attempt on a Life*

I'm restless. I can't sleep, I can't rest, I can't eat. I can't think either. I've changed clothes for the evening—changed into the darkest things I own to attract as little attention as possible. I've also found a scarf for my light hair, which is getting darker and darker along the part.

I've decided to go up to the studio at eleven. I more or less ran out of there this afternoon, but after getting hold of that picture, I knew I wanted to go up there.

I keep wondering where Rebecca got it. But I can't think. I've got to ask her, make her tell me. But there was something in her eyes…Right now I suspect everyone. I've hidden it away in my purse among my bills, my phantom bills. That's where it belongs.

It's already dark. The wind has changed course, and the swells hit the rock that the house is sitting on with a hollow sound.

There's also a motorboat somewhere down there, but I can't see it. The light is on over on Doreen's terrace, and it seems to me that the man I caught a glimpse of over there a moment ago was Rafael Vega.

I'm nervous. Even the water, which is running in the tank in the bathroom makes me tremble, so I get up on the toilet seat and adjust the mechanism. You have to do that every time, but I had forgotten. I don't feel like staying in the house. Instead I venture out in the streets and get farther out the main street than I've been before. Here I suddenly see the tall man dressed in gray who is always wandering around with the black book under his arm. He is sitting in a small office where there's room for him only.

His cap is lying on the table, and he sits there writing in his book, but when he discovers me, he comes to the door and signals to me that you're not supposed to walk any farther down the street toward what looks like a building site. I feel his eyes in my back until I find an alley so narrow I can hardly squeeze through. There is the smell of garbage.

The alley leads down to the square by the harbor but also farther out than I've been before, to the place where the big pier starts.

A smoking, black steamer is moored in front of a heap of coal. I'm somewhat surprised, because I don't know if that's the one I saw here on "my first evening" or if it's the one I saw as in a vision later on approaching the island with its extinguished lanterns in the moonlight. Across from the steamer there's a bar with lights behind colored glass panes. I hear guitar music and decide to go inside.

I suddenly see from out here, where there's less light than closer in toward the promenade, that there's something like a ball of light far away out over the sea as if from a town or another island.

Katy, Louisa, and Cora are in there. They look up as I step inside, but only Cora nods in my direction. Why?

They seem to be busy with something they've got in front of them on the table. Are they playing cards?

The man who is playing the guitar is blind. He sits there leaning against an enormous, bright column that supports the whole roof but that seems to come from another building. I want to sit down but discover there's a fourth glass on the girls' table. Maybe Dave is with them and plans to come back. I leave without ordering anything. As I shut the clattering, colored glass door behind me again, they laugh out loud, and their laughter goes right through me.

To prevent Dave from following me, I go into the first bar I see out here in these outermost, unfamiliar streets. There's a cellar where old men sit around playing the flute with one hand while beating a drum with the other. I can't stand the ear-splitting noise and decide to go into the next place, but there I catch sight of a red-faced, graying foreigner standing over by the counter. He is arguing with his wife, who screams and sobs and attacks him with her shoe while the blood flows from her nose. I've seen them before in the street. They are alcoholics.

In another place, also a cellar, it's quiet. The owners are an old couple, and they don't have any electric light. They put a candle on my table and bring me a glass of dark sherry; then they want to talk to me. They point to me and let me know they have seen me before, but I don't understand their language, so I just smile, shake hands with them, pay the bill, and leave.

I walk from one place to another trying to pass the time until it's eleven o'clock. One place I walk into is filled with barrels, but behind the bar there's a pale man gratuitously dressed in a raincoat as if it were the only article of clothing he owns. At one of the barrels Kellermann with his one arm is sitting with Marcel Chauvelot. At another, the Swede with the haggard face sits sleeping. Kellermann and Marcel Chauvelot stare at me and motion for me to come closer, but I pretend to be looking for someone who isn't there.

I escape into the next place, a large, vaulted cellar with yellow walls. It's Paco's place. There are lots of pictures everywhere—all of them portraits of Paco who is starting to play his guitar just now in the deep, damp silence between the clammy walls.

I look around. Everything is stained from dampness and darkened with age as if the place hadn't been touched for a hundred years. The only new things in it are the pictures of black Paco, the stained lamps, and the electric cords below the ceiling, which are black and fuzzy with flies that cannot get lose but are caught there every night when the lights are on.

I know quite a few of the people in here. I've seen some of them before.—Ruth Sherman is sitting by herself changing her facial expression according to the music, taking her glasses off and putting them on again, cleaning them. She's the one who applauds the loudest when Paco has finished a piece, but Ingrid, Britta, and "Mama," who is sitting by herself at another table, also applaud, for Paco plays well.

Some of the people don't applaud—like Deanson, his wife Marilyn, Juliette, and Nora. They are sitting at a distant table with a bottle in a cooler in the middle of the table, and they look as if their conversation has been interrupted by the music. Nora is pale with dark rims under her eyes, but, of course, that's the way women look sometimes. When Paco plays the next piece, which is announced by Ruth Sherman, she buries her head in her hands and remains sitting in this position long after it's over.

As I leave and get outside again, the light suddenly flickers in all the lamps as if they had caught fire, and then they go out all over town. That has happened before. There's a pale moon, which gives the plastered walls a bluish tint, and I see indistinctly a figure coming out of Paco's place and disappearing in the shadows. I think it was a man, but he walked faster than Deanson can walk. And Paco is lame. He has a club foot.

I consider going back in, but I've already made it quite far when the lights come on again. A strange feeling comes over me like a sneaking fear that I'm about to take leave of these streets. I suddenly notice the woman with the pain sitting there on her doorstep out toward the church square. She rocks from side to side while moaning softly. And all the children have disappeared tonight. Way up in the town a clock in a tower strikes ten, and the other clocks begin to answer until the deep bells boom right above my head and I start walking with quick steps in the direction of the large city gate with the headless figures.

But it's as if all the roads are blocked. At first I meet Federico, without his portfolio for once but with his cigarette and the scarf and the theatrical Apache cap that he always wears when he goes out. He looks upset and displeased and calls to me across the street:

"Don't go up in the upper part of town. There's no light."

As if he knew I was on my way up there! Incidentally he is right. The entire upper part of the town is in darkness.

The next person is Cora who asks me where I'm going and if I want to have dinner with her, and she has hardly let go of me before Mustapha pops up and—for the first time—begins speaking to me in his broken English, inviting me for a drink.

There's a raw energy about him that reminds me of something I've experienced and forgotten so that I can't formulate it in pictures and words but something I have retained a fear of deep within me. He has nothing to say to me. He just stands there staring at me as if I were a piece of white meat that he's got a hankering for.

I can tell from his breath that he's been drinking, and I have to use force to tear myself lose from his hands, which already have gotten hold of me.

He doesn't let go of me until Kieler, the photographer, walks past us; then I can walk on as I listen to their steps resounding on the tiles and eventually diminishing together with the pitiful howling of a dog that they have hurled stones after.

I'm just about to cross the market square to the ramp leading up to the large gate when I see Marcel Chauvelot sitting at a café table at the corner immediately below me and scouting the area with his hatchet face and his crooked neck as if he were waiting for someone.

It can't be Kellermann he is looking for, for Kellermann always sneaks up on him like a shadow that is gluing itself to its body. Is it I he is waiting for? Has he sent Kellermann off somewhere just because I happened to look into the bar where he was sitting and was obliged to nod to him, make excuses, in other words acknowledge his presence—so that he has gone out to look for me now?

But why is he sitting here, here of all places?

I stumble back through some other streets, stopping outside a small print shop with a thick book in the display window. While cooling my forehead on the pane, I wonder whether it was something

Sheila once said or if it's something I remember somehow from my unknown life: that in every one of the terrible camps they had during the last war they exterminated just as many people as there are letters in a book like that.

I try to imagine, but I can't. It's as if I'm trying to read a page in a book whose print flickers before my eyes, and suddenly I see a teeming city from high up above.

I go into a little bar where workers are eating and wash my face and my hands at the sink, which places like that always have.

I'm just about to sit down to have a glass of wine and a bite to eat, but now time is short.

I'm on my way up the path outside of town, the one I came down on from the French restaurant "my first evening."

I see through the windows that the cook is standing behind the kitchen counter as usual, but that Janine is exceptionally beautifully dressed as if she were going to a party. She has also cut her hair and changed her hairdo. I silently walk past the place, figuring that they don't see me or at least don't recognize me with the scarf around my head.

I have barely reached the next corner outside of the garden I came through that night—before I run into Rebecca. She is wearing new slacks and looks like a slender, handsome boy with her short hair, but her face is pale. She stops on the path when she sees me, her glance darting about perplexed, but she sees no way out and stays where she is till I catch up with her.

She knows what it is I want to ask her, and I can see she has already made up her mind not to tell me.

I take her hand, which feels cold.

"Where are you going, Rebecca?" I ask, and she looks down at the pavement with the smooth, round pebbles. But a few seconds later her glance moves upward, coming to rest on my sweater and then seeking my face. "Tell me, Rebecca! Who was it? Where did you find that picture? I've got to know."

She nods as if she understands that I have to know, but she says nothing.

"Where are you going, Rebecca?" I ask.

She points. "Down there. Janine has invited me." And suddenly she throws her arms around my neck.

"Oh, Miriam," she whispers, "I'm so afraid. I don't know what it is that's about to happen."

My fingers run through her thick hair as she clings to me.

"Is she the one?" I ask.

She shakes her head vigorously. "Won't you come with me, Miriam?" she whispers, tearing herself away from me and looking at me with shiny eyes.

"I can't now. Maybe later. Sure, if I can, I'll come a little later."

"Promise!"

"Yes," I say. I'm a bit confused, don't understand her eagerness. "I promise. But then you've got to tell me who it was."

Her eyes almost blind me on the dark path. It's as if something were rushing by in there in that part of her that always radiates the most, even though it's completely still and empty around us.

"It was Nora," she says quickly. "In a drawer. In her bedroom. The negative was there, too, but it was ruined."

Her eyes grow distant and inquisitive for a moment, then they suddenly hover right in front of my face, more radiant than ever: "Will you promise to come, Miriam?"

"Yes," I say, and we part with a handshake.

But I've gotten all the way up to the tunnel entrance above before I begin to understand—Rebecca!

I look down after her, but she is already out of sight.

I stand completely stiff so he won't notice me. I've almost reached the street leading to Don Ramon's studio when I catch sight of the red-haired painter coming out of there. He looks around to both sides and cuts across to some stairs leading down the slope.

Was it a trap up there—for me? Or for him? I try to think, but I can't think. There are too many unknowns in this comparison, one too many—me.

I'm dead tired. I lean against a wall as I watch his red head disappear down the stairs, bobbing down into the dark. The lights have come back on up here. Otherwise I would never have dared to walk through the tunnel with the iron grilles over there. But I'm so tired that all I want to do is just stand still and lean against the wall.

What is this mystery? Why did this have to happen? Why is he running down there in the dark, removing himself from me.—What do they know about me? I, who know nothing about myself. And who is this Henri anyway, who is the old painter, who is Sheila, and who is this red-haired man whom I feel I know more than ever before?—This movement of his, when he started running down the stairs, that rings a bell, I remember that—and I feel this scream inside me again that wants to come out but is stifled because I myself am about to suffocate.

"Michael!" I call. But he is already way down there, and it's as if I'm telling him everything—having a long conversation with him, during which I let him know that the others are waiting up there, but that I don't know what it's all about and that there's probably no point in my going up there since he, Michael, is the one I wanted to see.

Slowly I begin to walk down the stairs. I can see his head way down below as he walks past the lights. But a couple of minutes afterward I start running, staying in the shadows, for I hear footsteps and then a faint cry or an oath coming from the street up above where I was just standing.

He is all the way down at the end of the street where the stairs end, and I see him turning into the square. I run down a dark back alley in the same direction that he took, for I can hear the steps catching up with me in the dark.

Now I'm standing at the corner of the square. Hidden from view. At first I don't see him. The square is empty, and the pulse from the steam engine that powers the town's primitive generators thumps behind the houses and is noticeable in the lamps, which are getting whiter and whiter as always toward midnight, as I stand there listening and scouting.

The waiter is standing behind the glass door to the yellow bar, but nobody is sitting outside in the chairs, and over in the round, green kiosk it's deserted as well, except for two waiters in white jackets who are sitting there playing checkers.

The pulse from the engine is getting slower now, as always at this hour, while the lamps glow even whiter. Far away, a chorus of frogs is croaking, and I can hear the rumbling of barrels and tackles down by the harbor.

Way over at the outermost end of the square, a couple walking with their arms around each other disappear around a corner, and over behind the kiosk a priest walks by—I can see his black gown and hear his measured, resounding steps—but without looking around or entering the square. I'm still standing behind the corner in the shadows, and the only sound is the pulse, even more noticeable in the lamps now that it has slowed down, and a faint breeze up in the tree tops.

Then I suddenly see him. I see one of the dark silhouettes in the group of figures in the monument in the middle of the square moving slightly. The others are standing with rapiers and swords and carbines and large hats in the pulsating light, but now a figure with frizzy hair and a beard slowly emerges from the shadow of the middle plinth with a gun in his hand and slips in between the statues, where he stops and takes aim…

I get a side view of his pistol and know that it's not I he is aiming at. Then I see a flash behind him. As his gun drops, the figure falls while two, three, four shots resound from the alley on the opposite side, leading down to the street with the cars.

I want to rush forward, and my mouth is open as if I've already called his name, the name of the only person I recognize in this place and who is now lying doubled up over there, but I have not taken one step, have not stepped out of the shadows before two arms grab me and a wadded-up handkerchief is stuffed into my mouth.

It's Henri. At first he says nothing but just holds me tight like in a vice so that I can't move a muscle. Then he whispers:

"Don't move. Your life is at stake. Leave this scene as if nothing has happened and stay out of the light. Find a way home as if you were not coming from the square. Understand? I'll catch up with you in the main street."

He looks at me sternly and concerned; then he removes the gag.

"Yes, but Michael!" I gasp. "He's wounded, maybe…"

"Others will see to that…No one must know you saw him or witnessed this. Those were his own words. Hush!" He covers me completely with his enormous body so that the people rushing toward the monument don't see me.

I do as he says, and he gives me a little shove just before we turn into the alley where the house is. As we walk up the stairs and I hand him the key, he stops in surprise with a look of disbelief on his face.

Sheila is coming down the stairs from the floor above mine with a gun in her hand, which she is calmly aiming at us. Again her eyes have that little rapid movement from left to right from right to left, from one person to the other.

"Don't you think you owe us an explanation, Sheila?" Henri says, dangling the key in his hand.

"Don't move that hand," Sheila says hoarsely. "It's been a few years since I shot cigarettes out of people's fingers, and I'd just as soon not hurt you."

Her eyes continue their rapid movement. It's like the balance in a clock, and it's making me sick. But then she directs her glance first at Henri and then at me.

"We don't know a whole lot about each other on this island," she says. "Of course, that's the way things are here.—I'll take my chances and trust you, Henri. Maybe that's not taking too much of a chance, and maybe I'm insulting you unduly. Maybe that's what I've got to do in your case, too, Miriam, for I don't know you except the way we all know each other in this place where everything is over and nothing has yet begun.—But I know *him*. Where is…?"

"If you know him, then you'll be the best judge of whether or not you can help him," Henri interrupts. "He was shot over in the square before he himself had time to shoot. The place is crawling with people. And it's on his orders that I'm keeping her out of everything—maybe for your sake, too, for all I know."

Sheila is pale as a ghost, and her lifeless eyes glisten with tears. Her knuckles are white from clutching the banister. "Is he—?" she whispers, slowly lowering her gun with a gesture that was once part of her but has lost all meaning now.

"I don't know. You'll have to go yourself, Sheila," Henri says kindly but with an undertone of impatience. "I saw the gun fall at the first shot—far away from him."

"Thank God," Sheila mutters as she disappears down the stairs like a shadow.

—"She has searched your apartment!" is the first thing he says when we step inside and turn on the light.

The wardrobe is open, the bed has been torn apart, even the wood for the stove and the paper and the groceries in the green cabinet have been moved around. "Yes," I say, wanting to say more, but he stops me.

"Don't try to talk," he says. "Get some rest! I'll sleep here on the couch. Tomorrow you'll be sensible and think hard and then come out to my place. Do you know where it is?"

I nod. He is right.

But when I stand in the bathroom a little later, I know there's one thing he's not right about.

The water in the tank is running again. Someone has used the toilet. There were only two sheets of paper left, and they just covered the cardboard roll this morning. Now there's only one.—Something like that women do automatically.—But when I examine the wooden seat, which is new and painted white, there are no scratches. And Sheila always wears a girdle and hose when she goes out at night.

I never do myself, and lots of women don't, but I can't make myself explain that to this man who measures over six feet in his stocking feet and who is standing outside the door handing me a glass of my own cognac.

CHAPTER EIGHT · *In the Empty House*

When I wake up, Henri has left. I've slept soundly, and it crosses my mind that he may have put something in my cognac. But it's more likely because he was there that I could sleep, for once just sleep and give in to this never-ending fatigue.

It's all gone once I'm fully awake and remember what happened. I quickly get dressed and am already on my way out the door to Henri's when I remember the photograph.

I close the door again and sit down in the room on the sea with "Anthony's" picture in front of me on the table. Didn't Henri tell me to think hard? And I do think, but it's like before a move in a game of chess where I don't know the names or the value of the pieces and where I'm simply being chased across the squares on the board without being able to protect myself and without knowing why I'm being chased—not to mention why they want to kill the only person I feel certain I know. The only person.

The only person from the period prior to when I woke up in this room a few days ago.

I stare at the picture in front of me, and I lower my eyes, for even behind the glossy exterior of the photograph these eyes are too strong for me, but not as strong as they are in reality, because in that case they would not permit me to feel this wave of hatred that is rising in me, rising to such an extent that I know nothing could stop me…and I'm amazed and horrified at myself!

I hear Sheila's voice again saying: "We don't know a whole lot about each other on this island!— Of course, that's the way things are here…where everything is over or nothing has yet begun!"

I see in front of me the faces I've met here, one by one: Sheila, Dave, Nora, Federico; Mustapha's which makes me shiver, Marcel Chauvelot's which makes me freeze with fear—all the women, the artists, the older men, Maritza, all of them: They are all strangers, and I hear the voice again…

I put my hands up to my ears to keep from hearing their voices and from hearing the sea while I frantically look for a way out. But I just keep seeing, over and over again—just like "the other morning" when I kept seeing the moment before me when I met Sheila—keep seeing the silhouette of the painter falling off the monument and hearing the gun hitting the pavement in the empty square.

I also see Henri, worried and looking sternly at me again while he holds me tight as in a vice. And I don't know why, but suddenly Nora is staring at me as well with her eyes, which are yellow, as she laughs and sticks her tongue out between her teeth, her strange eyes which suddenly turn black again…

I get up. I know what I've got to do. I find a pencil and write "Miriam" on the photograph in the same print that was used for the other words so that it now reads: FOR MY DARLING MIRIAM FROM "ANTHONY." There are no letters I haven't been able to copy.

I put it in my purse, and suddenly I don't understand how I've been able to sit here so long. I'm overcome again with this unpredictable and somewhat foolish indignation toward Henri because he is different from the rest and because he has ordered me to sit here and think when I don't know if Michael, at whose request (—?) Henri took care of me, is dead or alive.

Michael has been hurt—his hand and his shoulder, but not seriously. Everyone is talking about the strange assassination attempt, so I don't need to ask. He has been hospitalized at the clinic.

Sheila is nowhere to be found, but when I walk past the clinic, I see her car pulling up, stopping at the rear entrance, and Sheila, Rafael Vega, and a uniformed man getting out.

They go into the clinic. The uniformed man comes out again, starts the car, and returns a few minutes later with one more guard. There's one at every entrance now, and they are armed.—At the end of the road where I'm standing lies the area with the canals where the fat smiling woman gave me the large wax flower that first evening. There are many paths, and I can't see which one of the sheds over there is hers.

Way over there, Rebecca walks by. I think she sees me, but she turns her face away and walks on. I feel hurt.

The day is hot and clear. It marches forward like

one of these large clock hands—in little jerks as if no moment were linked to the next or to the one that just was.

I go up to talk to Nora.

At the entrance to the courtyard with the noseless lions I run into Dave.

He's happy to see me and asks if I want to go for a swim. He says he's got money and wants us to have lunch together.

I shake my head. "Later, Dave, maybe later," I lie, "Or another day," and I don't know if maybe I even mean it:—just to wake up and get out of bed and go swimming and have lunch while you talk about the weather—or the assassination attempt—and then that's the whole day.

"You're so sweet," he says.

"Thanks," I say.

"I felt kind of resentful toward you the other day. Please forget it."

"Sure," I say. "Maybe it was my fault. But tell me something, Dave," I say sharply, because now he's going to have to answer me. "You haven't seen that picture of Anthony anywhere, have you? It

264

must be one of those crazy girls who bought it. The negative is gone, too, and now I remember he asked me to send it. He needs it, and I'm going to be in trouble, you know." I look straight at him.

He shakes his head. His dark blue eyes are handsome when he is sober and feels like going swimming.

"No, I haven't seen hide nor hair of it," he says. "But I'll be sure to let you know if I see it anywhere. Sure you don't want to come along?"

I shake my head no and stubbornly keep talking the way a girl on "La Isla" supposedly talks:

"Seeing anything of Rebecca these days, I mean, more intimately?"

"No," Dave says, "and, by the way, I think she may be on the wrong team now.—Well, I've got to run, bye bye! And take care now!"

It's as if I have two hearts, two quite ordinary young girl's hearts, as I walk up the chipped marble stairs to the mansion, and both of those hearts hurt unbearably. And where is that third heart, my strong courageous heart, which I need so badly for what lies ahead of me now?

It's only eleven, but there's already a cocktail party at Nora's. They are all there, all the ones you would expect to see here.

I decide to join the party while waiting for a chance to talk to Nora. She has already handed me a glass and is now showing off the new, low-cut blouse she is wearing, which accentuates the fine curve of her neck and shoulders, as well as an amethyst she has had affixed to a Chinese snake ring. She is very chic, and she laughs with her yellow eyes, which are farther apart than I remember, laughs so that her tongue forms a little cup when I admire her purple Indian slippers with their gold pattern matching her bracelet. She is wearing her hair in a frizz, and her ears are faintly pink like a child's, forming the backdrop for the two black pearls she has put in them. But her black jeans are much too tight for her thick waist, and I notice the lines on her neck and on her heavy eyelids. She is not as young as she looked at first glance.

It is empty in Nora's apartment as it is everywhere else in the old mansion: Just a couple of couches, a dozen colorful pillows, and some mats along the wall. On the other hand, there's a genuine bar in one corner, where Mustapha, quite professional looking with a dish towel over his shoulder, is mixing drinks. He gives me a quick look, baring his white teeth. I shudder and gratefully join Ruth Sherman, who is calling me from her pillow in the middle of the floor, from where the "action paintings" on all the walls look like frozen or overgrown window panes.

I also see the crack running down the length of the ceiling and the end walls.

"Isn't that dangerous?" I say pointing to it.

"Sure," Ruth answers, "but Nora arrived late, about the time you did, I think, so she had to take what she could get.—As a matter of fact, we're all wondering how Anthony managed to arrange for you to stay in the big house. I hear they're tearing it down.—Don't you miss him?" she continues.

"Oh yes," I say. "I sure do.—What's Mustapha doing here?" I ask to get her off the subject.

"He's always here. Didn't you know? He's got a room over there—," she points, "next to Dave's. They have their own entrance from some other part of the house, too. Isn't this a neat house?"

I nod.

"And these parties people throw when you least expect them!" she continues. "Like today after that awful assassination attempt—they say it's smugglers who are making war on each other!—I think it was arranged last night, the party, but many of us didn't hear about it until this morning down in the town. Do you know everyone? I don't think you've seen that fellow over there before. His name is Hanson, and his wife was murdered by a thrill killer where he comes from. That's why he always walks around with this briefcase under his arm with all the pictures of her and the clippings relating to the case."

She points to the pale Swede whom I already know. He is sitting there with his briefcase.

"That's terrible," I say. "Like walking around with her ashes; I mean, it's even worse."

"It's perverse," Ruth Sherman says.

Hanson! So now I have a name for him, one more name to remember in this place where you either remember nothing or remember only too well. Who was it that said that a couple of days ago … ?

I look around. It looks like they are all here, except for Sheila and Rebecca. I see Deanson and Marilyn, William Vickers Adams and Juliette, and the married couple that had that fight in the bar last night. She's got a band-aid under her eye.

"Who's that?" I whisper.

"That's the Dobsons, Commander Dobson and his wife. They lost four sons in the war, that's why they always drink and argue. They blame each other. He was in the military, you know, and she was in politics." Ruth is the blue book of this place.

Along the one wall, I see Katy and Louisa and Diana. The Swedish women are not here, nor is Ingrid who otherwise is always seen with Mustapha. I don't know why I notice.

Frankie and Leslie have gotten interested in "action painting" and are walking from picture to picture discussing them. Some of the pictures must be theirs, because I see them scratching them with their nails and gouging them with a comb.

Wally is sitting alone watching them disapprovingly, and next to her are the Japanese, standing silent and polite as always with soft drinks in their glasses. The veteran with the horrible face is sitting in the darkest corner, and just now Federico is making his entrance together with Maurice and Doreen. They look around as if they had come too early and would just as soon leave again.

269

Everyone—with the exception of the Japanese—is on his second drink since I came, and the atmosphere is great. Frankie and Leslie have taken one of their "action paintings" down from the wall and are having fun improving on it by splattering it with ink from a fountain pen.

Then I hear Tubby's deep tuba voice from the door. He starts to speak even before he has entered the room, and today he needs no encouragement, no contrary point of view, no conversation. He's in full command.

"Now, just take a look at those chicks over there who aren't even chicks. Look how they are playing with these blobs which they think are blobs but which are really eyes staring at them from out of chaos, eyes that will always be there if they happen to shake their hand or make any sort of movement. Just like the eyes that fear used to stir in you when you walked through a forest when you were little…"

Someone finds him a crate, and he sits down perspiring, with his cane next to him. He continues to hold forth, and at first everyone listens except the two boyish girls who deliberately continue what they are doing. But after a while they are all wrapped up in their own affairs again, and Tubby's deep bass is both like the echo of and commentary on everything that's being said and done here in this room, too deep to be heard if you weren't paying attention. An octave deeper than everything else being said.—I cling to this voice which says what cannot be said—straining to hear it through the din while I wait. Wait.

"Look at them…These so-called artists have been trying for the longest time to offend the middle class, to hit where it hurts…now there's no one left to offend…now they are alone…now they begin themselves, the little ones!

"And when they have gotten tired of that, as they have gotten tired of sex—on one side or the other— then they no longer know what they want…until war comes and ravages them and they realize that's what they want. But they probably have a hopelessly antiquated notion about that. They forget that Leviathan is already standing guard, encircling the planet, winding in and out every minute of the day so that no one can ever point to it and say: there it is!—and that the projectiles are spewed forth like worms from its eyes…

"Do you know who they are, the ones sitting over there, those whom life has invited to dance and who are now left sitting here? They are the ones who said that 'the ways of the beetle are more beautiful than a sonata by Mozart!' They are the ones who believed in a religion of development and progress which was to 'sanctify the higher manifestations of the human spirit' in art and in love and emphasize the meaning of life's being lived to the fullest in every respect and with all its possibilities…They are the ones who thought they could foresee the inhabitants of the earth getting so far as to communicate with each other by means other than just words… just think, how prophetic! Cheers!

"They are the ones who honor the scientists, indeed, worship these brains with their peculiar and impersonal talent, those who for the most part are satisfied with their jobs and have been so caught up in them that they don't need to think but let *the jobs* do the thinking for them—indeed, who don't even need to think about the short time that has passed since science was something you tinkered with on the living room table after it was cleared, as I seem to recall. These stalwart students who, if they are well meaning enough and brought up in the tradition of old-fashioned humanism, as Einstein was, find to their dismay one day that they don't have one word of comfort to give to anyone. But there aren't even too many left of those…"

Tubby perspires and drinks. Wally has moved over by him and is sitting there listening like me.

"And what about you, Tubby?" she asks, stroking her forehead and her hair nervously and hard.

"I'll tell you, my child, my little Germanic portrait sculpture," he says. "I'm ill and mad now just like the others, and you know why, but I was one of those who wanted to 'improve the world and renew life in all its cultural aspects through the labor unions.' As soon as the unions had met their reasonable demands for salaries in proportion to the cost of living, they would become guilds and brotherhoods again just like in the Middle Ages and be responsible for their products in the same manner. Work would be transformed into active happiness! All the workers of the world would unite and block the road for the warlords. Art was to experience a rebirth—how about that!—Even language was to find new frontiers, new radiant words and incomparable imagery to describe this great new age where new art forms would arise through mass communication. And who were the ones that believed in this with me? You won't believe your own ears, because they are still living. Are you listening, are you listening, you who are sitting here with me!—It's those names that first come to mind, even though you haven't read any books here on the island for many years."

"Yeah, it's strange," I say to Wally. "No one seems to read here."

"It's because of our nerves," Wally says. She is supporting Tubby who has collapsed and has a streak of saliva running down his chin. "It's just like Berlin back then. It was the same thing there."

"Not newspapers either?" I ask carefully.

"Oh, sure, we used to get some. Sheila used to get quite a few from the outside. But we haven't received any in the last couple of months because of the present situation."

"Present situation?"

"Well, war was about to break out again, you

know, and we are neutral here and under double censure. That's what I heard anyway."

—The whole room is suddenly silent, and something is about to happen to me. I had the same feeling the other night here in this house when I was together with these people; but it's clearer, harsher now in the light of day:—I'm sitting high up in a room, a tower, whose pictures—which are windows—face death and frost and chaos. Mold and decay push up against the windowpane outside, or ghastly colored clouds conceal the countries of the earth; and all the people who are here in this room with me high above "La Isla" are like shadows. I can see through them now—now that the sun is breaking through from elsewhere with its corrosive rays while millions and more millions of creatures move and glisten in the sunbeam…

—Then I hear Nora's voice: "Looks like we've got enough cars. Maurice is getting a few more. So we'll go out to the caves today since it's so hot. Don't forget to take your glasses with you, and you guys each bring a bottle."

I have no other recourse than to go along if I want to talk to her.

"There's Mars in broad daylight!" says Wally, who is standing by the open window looking out toward the town. "Did you know that the canals up there have changed a lot? I remember quite a bit about it, and I borrowed Nora's binoculars one day. Some people think they are plants and others that they are sand, but no one can figure out why the lines are so even."

"They are ants," Tubby mutters, "—of sorts!"

CHAPTER NINE · *The Cave*

A stupid little meaningless word keeps pounding in my temples, stretching the artery around my skull like a singing string. It's the word "sensible." I promised Henri to be sensible and think hard.

And now I'm caught in a trap.

I know that, although nothing has happened yet.

The others have just gone outside in the warm sun. I heard the sound of cars starting and driving off.

But Nora shouted, "You're going with us! I took your purse and put it in my car!"

—So she knows which purse is mine! This minute she is standing with it outside. Standing with the picture of "Anthony." And outside suddenly seems so far away. And who is "us"? That must be she and Mustapha. He drove her car out here.

I look around this trap that I'm caught in and that was laid with me in mind. Like how many other things here?

The grotto is large and deep. A few feet away some primitive stairs lead down to a darkness which you can't see the bottom of, and everywhere the gnarled, grayish walls glisten with dampness. Here and there I hear water dripping—to this day, after thousands of years, in the process of forming these grayish phallic columns that rise from the ground, so lifelike in their dead whiteness. And in one place I hear water trickling in a fine stream.

"Sensible," something hammers in my temples, something sings in my taut, aching artery: "Sensible! There's water! You won't die of thirst! Just don't look around and let fear get hold of you! Watch out that you don't fall so that artery starts to bleed, so that frail, aching skull with its thin layer of skin…"

…Quiet. There she stands. She has just come in from the outside, and she can't see me yet, for her eyes, her yellow cat's eyes, are blinded by the light out there.

She doesn't say anything, but she holds the photograph in her hand, and I can see her eyes looking for me in the darkness.

If I could just…reach the wall, squeeze into a

niche and stand there like a madonna of fear with the water trickling down over me. But she will see my movement the moment I take just one single step, see my light shirt under which my heart is beating so my bosom shakes…

In another second she is bound to see me.

Should I try to escape anyway? Or should I throw a rock and try to hit her? But why?—Maybe she is armed and the other person is waiting out there. The other person.

Should I try anyway? I bend down carefully and pick up one of the slimy rocks, a little broken-off column shaped like the big gray ones.

Now she's getting closer. Did she see me move?

I raise my arm ready to throw, but at that moment she herself moves, uttering a sort of scream, while her face turns so indescribably horrible in the gray-green light from the wet walls above her.

I'm paralyzed. I can't throw. I'm frantic as well. Is that a gun she's got in her hand?

Her face is a mask of hatred. It's green and yellow with smoking black eyes as if she were a part of the walls. As if she…belonged here in the cave.

Suddenly I see what it is she's doing: She has

crumpled up the photograph, and now she is tearing it to shreds. I want to call to her, but I can't call to that face; and the other—the other person has appeared behind her now. Finally, finally my legs obey, and I run, stumbling and sliding on the slimy floor, trying to grab hold of the rocks, these stony warts that fill my hands. I hear how he, too, runs forward but is blinded so that he, too, falls. I manage to get myself up and crawl on my stomach over to the stairs leading down to the darkness so that he won't see me.

And just as the last glimmer of daylight disappears, as I crawl backward down into the darkness, I hear her calling:

"Damn, damn, damn! Damned in all eternity! Find her...do with her what you want!"

There's only a weak, greenish glow above the place where his head now appears. He can't see me yet, as I work my way down toward the bottom. It won't be long before I'm done for.

But just as he catches a glimpse of me—it must be my hair, because I'm completely gray and grubby and slimy all over my body, and I cover my hair with slime, too, so that he won't see me—just at that moment my feet hit a ledge in the rock. There's darkness even farther down, and maybe there's water as well. It's so strangely loud, and it makes me wonder, because it's as if moss is growing down here…I feel something soft around my feet, and I suddenly see a weak glimmer of daylight through a crack, toward which I must make my way forward on my stomach. But it's only when I have reached a larger cavity where one of the rocks I'm reaching for is a lizard scurrying away, and the walls around me look like faces that have never come to life although some kind of life is stirring in every nook and cranny…only then do I realize that the soft mass I stepped in was not moss at all. Instead I'm fuzzy all over with long-legged insects which cover the rocks where I came from like a living fur and which now cover me…

My scream must have made them think I had plunged to the bottom. For I'm alone when I wake up. He did not follow me although I expect to see his face appearing out of the darkness any moment covered with living fur.

Most of the insects have scattered, but I bite my lip so it bleeds every time I crush them with my hands and find them underneath my clothes. Then I have to defend myself again, because they go for my blood, and I have to brush them away from my eyes and my ears. I twist this way and that, ridiculously, like a wounded fish, while hitting my elbows and knees till they bleed, as I move toward the strip of daylight I can see.

For a moment I think I can't squeeze through or that the large chunks of rock hanging above me will come tumbling down and crush my back if I continue to crawl between the already fallen chunks, which become more numerous and tear away at me till I bleed.

But finally my hand reaches out for grass and plants, and I see trees.

I'm free.

CHAPTER TEN · *The Hermit*

I ease forward on my stomach through the grass, and only after a long time has gone by does it occur to me that I can stand up now. But I lie down again right away and listen.

It's quiet here. There's no one around. The entrance to the cave is far away on the other side of the rock at whose foot I'm lying like a grimy mess.

The highway runs all the way over there among the trees, and once in a while a car passes by, but always in the direction of town.

I wait for half an hour or more, for a long time. Not a sound. No footsteps. They must have left.

They think I've plunged into the darkness and disappeared forever…

Why? Even after *this* I don't know why. Why are they hounding me? Who am I?—and what do they want with me? Why am I here? What is this island, "La Isla"? And who are they?

Quiet. Don't think now. My limbs hurt. The

wounds on my elbows and knees sting. My mouth is bleeding, and my tongue is thick from thirst even though I'm lying in the shade.

A grimy mess. I run my hand through my slimy hair and find yet another half-dead insect.

I shiver and bury my face in the grass, inhaling its cool dampness and digging my fingers down under it as if I wished to be a plant, as if I needed to find that energy which exudes from the soil.

For how else will I get my energy? I have to crawl out into the sun. I have to reach the highway farther out and get across it. I'm pretty sure that's where Henri's house is located.

I wait one more minute. I'm dead tired. But as I stare down into the grass, I notice it's full of tiny creatures that I didn't see before.

Everywhere from the long, shiny leaves and from the corners where they emerge from the darkness, masks stare at me. Or an insect moves, a light-yellow one or a silver-gray one or just now a grass-green one encumbered by and caught in a peculiar, exotic technique that has become part of it.

Images of fear, masks more horrifying than in any jungle. Strange, soulless eyes and jaws and stingers and spears, which I'm protected against only because of my relatively colossal size here and now.

I rise up halfway, lying on my aching knees like a shade-giving cloud above the grass, whose creatures are now so far away that I can't make them out without straining my eyes.

The shapes of fear. Worms like entrails that have wriggled away from a larger animal; caterpillars like visions of a technique from some strange planet where the sun is never seen and the wheel is not known; spider webs—the invisible will made visible in beauty like crystals, only stretched in front of claws and jaws, in front of that mask of terror which is hidden now just because it's too small for me to see from here. And now the flies arrive, blue and green, shiny like metal as if they were just turned out and let loose on their victim, which is also me, a stinking pile tempting them with slime and wounds and trickling blood.

They buzz around me. But there's also another buzzing sound. Is it a plane? It's a deep and terrible sound that becomes louder and louder, and I'm seized with an unutterable fear as I turn and look after it with smarting eyes. *For it is larger than I, this sound*—I think, and I'm at its mercy if it comes too close with its noisy rotor and these windows that are like the eyes of flies (—that's how it was, I remember, but where?)…and even if I could make myself tiny, I would be among the same beings, the same kind that are now hiding and buzzing down in the grass…

Even in the cave earlier I didn't experience any greater fear than what I'm feeling now—on my knees in the grass, a refugee between two realms of terror and fear. The high-pitched sound of cicadas from the sunshine out there is like all the acute stabbing pain contained in my human body right now, and not just in my body either.

There must be at least a hundred cicadas. They started just before when the sun reached them. But they are invisible, invisible. Like the pain that is stabbing me (From where? Why?)…

There wasn't any plane. It was two large motorcycles racing by over on the road. I don't know what made me think of a plane just now. Am I expecting one? Here?

Have I been out here before, by the caves, in the

caves? They were not unfamiliar…No, don't think, don't think now, it will only turn into delirium! I must crawl, I must start to crawl out into the sun, out among the cicadas, over toward the road far away over there.

The grass pricks and cuts. It's dry here, and there's stubble sharp as glass. And still this high-pitched sound coming from nowhere. I'm in the middle of the savanna of olive trees with the reddish soil, and my hands and knees are red with soil and blood.

There haven't been any cars over on the road for a long time, but when one does come, I lie down flat and wait till it's out of sight. The sun bakes, and my tongue swells. Maybe I bit it? Or an insect has…I sob, but my sobs only turn into stinging hiccups.

It must still be siesta time when people stay inside. If only Henri is home! I become more and more certain that he lives over there on the other side of the road.

Here and there, there are twigs and tree roots like disintegrating beings that haven't gotten out of the sting of the sun in time, have not been able

287

to save themselves.

And there—isn't that a shadow, a back over there? Paralyzed with fear, I lie down flat, and freeze right there in the sunshine. My heart hammers away so that I think it can be heard all the way over by the road.

But it's a cat…just a cat. When was it I also met a cat? It seems so long ago.

It stares at me in fixed surprise and watchfulness out of its velvet mask. Then it bares its teeth—as a warning, a little white gleam—and disappears. All the rest of the way through the endless field of stubble, I have to close my eyes every second, because I see all kinds of animals in front of me that I may only have read about or seen pictures of or seen in a zoo once, enormous beasts from the large continent, from Africa's savannas over there beyond the sea…They come stomping across me, and I see their backs, and I don't want to meet their gaze and see their horns of power and trunks and masks of cunning but bury my face in the red gravel between the pricking straws. Finally I calm down again and drag myself the last stretch out to the road.

I lie in the ditch listening and looking and then run across the road bent over forward with a little cloud of dust around my feet and down the red path to the blinding wall, to Henri's house, which looks like a pure white loaf of bread that the sun has baked.

I hammer frantically at his door. Then I don't remember anything…

It's white and yellowish here, bright. The white is plastered, textured walls, and the yellow is unpainted wood. The bed I'm lying in is of light, unpainted wood as well.—He must have undressed me and washed and bandaged me, for all I have on is a large, brown bathrobe, completely covering my hands and feet, and I feel the bandages tight around my elbows and knees. With some difficulty I manage to get my sleeves cuffed so that I can move my hands. They are red with iodine, and I've got a bandage around one of my wrists. I feel my hair. It's wet, and I've got a towel under my head.

"You were a sight to behold!" he says as he comes into the room.

I try to smile. It hurts.

"Did I pass out?" I can't raise my voice above a whisper.

"Yes, from exhaustion," he says. "You've been sleeping."

I don't know what to say. It's bright inside me, warm yellow and white with a touch of sun, just as it is in the room. I don't want to talk about what happened, not just now, not about the darkness, about…I don't have the strength. Then my eye falls on a tall slender vase, a Greek amphora completely overgrown with snails and mussels, leaning against the wall in the corner. It's the only thing in the room except for some books lying on the table.

"Does that come from the sea?" I ask.

"Yes," he says. "In a way. It comes from the cave where you were. It was a sea bottom once." He stands there in the doorway watching me with these multi-colored eyes that have a little light, blue flower closest to the pupil.

"Tell me what you remember," he says, but when he sees my fear, he immediately continues, "No, not that. We'll get to that later. Tell me what you remember from before. And drink this!"

He hands me a glass of cold tea that's been standing ready on the table for me, covered with a book.

"But I don't remember anything at all," I say when I've had something to drink. "I don't even know who I am.—And I don't know who you are either!" I say, suddenly upset, "and if you know something, if you, too, are hiding something from me…" I have raised myself halfway up to get out of bed but fall back again. I'm too exhausted, and the tears throb behind my eyeballs, but this time it's because I had doubts, so much so that my happiness vanished.

Again he has this stern and worried look.

"Tell me what you remember, *Ann Mary,*" he says gently, "since you…woke up here on the island."

I stare at him. That's it! That's my name, Ann Mary, I know it is. But how does he know?

"Do I have to?" I whisper. "Why…?"

"It's the best way," he says, and I tell him.

A long time has passed, during which the shadows of the olive trees outside have moved and grown longer and the sun has left the room. After I've had some more tea, I say after a long pause, "And then we reached the cave—." He stops me and comes over and sits down by me.

"It's as if I can't get away from that cave. It's as if I'm still down there—or out there in the sun among the insects," I whisper, squeezing his hand. "If I only could get it out of my mind."

"You can't get it out of your mind," he says calmly, "but if you understand it, you can deal with it. That's why you don't need to tell me about it, not yet."

"What is it that's happening?" I whisper, looking over at the amphora that has come from the deep just like me.

"*Who* comes to mind just now as you're saying that?" There's something urgent in his voice, and his eyes are earnest and mild, but the little blue flower deep inside has closed up. It's getting dark outside.

"I don't know," I say. "I'm pretty sure I'm thinking about the bishop, about Gallus and the bishop. That was so awful what he said. Is he right?"

There's an energy emanating from him as he sits there listening—also for what I'm not saying or can't express. He could make me forget, I'm sure of that. But instead he wants me to remember—

something else.

"They're probably both right," he says slowly, looking out the window where the gray olive trees have turned red from the setting sun. "It depends on what they are paying for it, how they are living it or will live it. Maybe Gallus has paid more than the bishop after all—with his uncertainty. They are like two different ages when they meet. But that's exactly the way it should be."

"But you," I say, "what do you think? You never say anything. Don't you believe in the Church?"

He looks seriously at me. Then he walks over and lights a candle in a candlestick and puts it on the table.

"The Church is a vision," he says. "A vision that a few men once had. Since then the vision took *form*, towering in an age when everything was stone and body and there were many who lived in it."

"But the others, the ones Gallus talked about, the future that will come, these teeming masses in the new age?"

He is silent for a long time; then he goes and gets another candle and puts it on the table.

"Who knows if the future might not be a past as

293

well," he finally says. "A past where what is thought without being understood is irresistibly created in its own will. Those buildings that are going up now were dreamed up in the foxholes during the first world war. Did you ever hear of an architect by the name of Mendelssohn?"

I shake my head.

"Who knows if it isn't at the very moment when we understand it and see it before us with human eyes that we own the age that began then? In any case, that's one possibility we have, but if we don't see it clearly, this age will take us with it, and we'll disappear with its generations, die with it, defenseless, that part of us that can die."

"What cannot die?" I seek his eyes, and my voice is a whisper.

"Pain cannot die! The pain at not having seen, which is greater than the pain that comes from seeing. Therefore we must suffer that pain."

"Like Tubby?" I say. "Do you know Tubby?"

"Yes." Henri suddenly smiles, and the light glistens in his overly large hair and his strangely angular eyebrows. "He thinks the Earth is dying, and I sometimes think that my only raison d'être may be my ability to convince him of something else someday."

"What would you convince him of?" My voice is hoarse, but now it's with emotion. His words have affected me and don't leave me in peace.

"Maybe of the fact that it's a heaven that is dying instead and that it's only now that we're about to live on Earth."

"What do you mean? A heaven—?" I almost shout.

"I mean the East," he says firmly. "It's the dead heavens you see there now—with dark figures on the thrones ruling their millions soon to become billions—but all of them are just images of human beings."

"Images of human beings?"

He looks out into the darkness outside, and I follow his glance. I see only our own reflections in the pane. Then he says, as if he were talking to the darkness out there, "They think two human beings can give birth to a whole world, populating the Earth and making it their possession. But they are mistaken. For it's life alone that can spawn image after image of us without our ever being able to understand it or having claims to anything at all.—We are born in images. Didn't you ever think about that when you walked around in there in the streets?"

I nod.

"You see, it's inevitable. The town in there is an ancient town, and in antiquity there were no human beings yet in spite of myths and dreams of human beings. There were only sons and daughters, a principle of life that became flesh and blood just like the Church became stone. But in the East they are building ancient kingdoms now since the world of antiquity is dead because its gods are dead, and—just like the hermit crabs do—others have taken their shape and their space—and rule!"

"And the West?" I ask, for I'm beginning to suspect that he has a purpose with these words which I will know this evening still or tonight and which concern me personally, me Ann Mary. I listen, and he fixes me with his gaze.

"In the West we still have the possibility of understanding ourselves. Here we do not live in the dead heavens. Here it is the underworld rising around us like noisy markets or magic cities and nights; but even if we can be tempted, after all, we don't have to surrender to them. We draw our paths among them, and it's as if these paths draw the picture of one enormous face which is that of man."

"Which arises from that which we are living?" I say softly.

"Yes, which soon will exist and start to speak," Henri says looking into the flame. "Whatever was said in books that no one read just a few years ago is now being written in the newspapers. Even those wars and horrors and catastrophes that arose in the West have been curtailed, if you think about it, have become images, horrible images to be sure—visions and nightmares in which a lot of people perished but out of which our consciousness arose so that we can sit here talking as we are doing just now. We just need time, but we need that more than anything else. Then someday we'll understand."

"But just what can we do?" I ask in a low voice. It is completely dark now. The two candles are reflected in his eyes and shine on my face, which I meet again inside his black pupils as they look at me.

"We must learn how to feel," he says. "Think of Greece where ideas were robbed like jewelry from the raiments of the gods—and still they could not feel. Feelings were the characters of mythology, three or four, simple ones like the music of those days. Hence the masks of tragedy. Hence, later, the brutality of the gladiator fights, the verity of atrocities, the bonfires of the martyrs and the expressionless faces of the Middle Ages that were looking on!" He clenches his broad, slightly hairy hand. "It's as if some individuals from these multitudes are now coming into existence again—after Dostoyevsky, after Beethoven! And they will sacrifice just as people did in Antiquity and during the Middle Ages. They will sacrifice others, never anything in themselves—" he looks at me, a long, searching glance between the candles "—like us!"

At that moment I am certain I hear a plane above the island. The sound comes quite close for a moment and then disappears again. I listen, meeting his eyes. He has heard it, too, but doesn't say anything. It is quiet again.

"Like us?" I say hesitantly.

"Yes, because now the myths are becoming real through us. Now we'll have a chance to own them—and not they us—if we're willing to pay.— Look at your sister, the amphora there in the corner. Wasn't it lost and then saved from the deep of the sea!"

"Like me?" I say, taking a deep breath.

"Like you," he says. "Now you can tell your story."

I tell him, and I don't notice how badly my hand hurts when I squeeze his.

"Must we always pay with suffering?" I ask afterward.

"Yes, with the willingness to suffer," he says quietly, looking away, and I feel as if my eyes are ready to make a promise but that he won't accept that.

"Why are you leading me into this?" I say to his back. "Isn't it enough that wars and earthquakes and death are coming? Why must we always think of suffering?"

"We don't understand these catastrophes, of course," he says. "They only negotiate with us. They are often just the conclusion to what was not understood. But they, too, are about to enter our consciousness. In the old days probably no one thought we ourselves would cause the Flood or Armageddon—or that we might stop them precisely because we understand them!"

"But why not?" I say desperately in this silent house. "Even if I, too, were willing, why all this suffering?"

His face is dead serious when he answers, "Because there is One who is suffering—in us—so that man may live. Because since He lived, the Earth has become a place in eternity where His spirit lives while Heaven is dying and its reflections on Earth are withering. We are alone with the One who can conquer death. That's my belief."

I feel his eyes resting on me, and it is silent in the room for a long time. The candles are burning without a sound.

"But happiness?" I finally say. "All the things that make life worth living."

"When was the last time you were happy?" he asks.

"I guess I don't remember," I mutter vaguely. "Oh yes," I say hesitantly, "it was when I woke up here before. Everything was so bright!"

Now he smiles and goes out to get us something to eat, and while we eat, I hear a distant, muffled bang. He walks outside to look, and when he comes back, I see lines of worry on his forehead.

"What was it?" I ask.

At first he doesn't answer, but then he mutters, "I have a feeling we'll know very soon."

He walks over and bolts the door. Then he closes the shutters, goes and gets a lamp, and sits down by me to check my bandages. They are quite professional, and his hands with the light hair and the smooth, taut skin examines my calves and knees, bending and stretching my leg, calmly and professionally, almost appraisingly. I also notice an open medicine kit over on the table now where a syringe lies ready for when I go to sleep.

"Are you a doctor?" I ask surprised.

He nods and smiles. For a moment there's something boyish about his smile.

"I was," he says, "but now I'm on 'La Isla,' of course, and I haven't decided yet if I want to be a doctor again."

"Isn't it lonely for you here?" I ask.

"'La Isla' is also *my* stay of execution, you know,"

he says almost cheerfully. "There comes a day when one must make an effort to understand all the blunders one has made." He is done with the other leg and knee now and tucks me in again. Then he examines my wrist, which disappears in his large hand as he bends it. "And besides, someone happens to have found her way out here," he says looking at me.

—The next moment I watch my hands convulsively grabbing hold of his sleeve, for a car has stopped out in the road, and I hear footsteps running up the path and someone hammering at the door.

I feel nauseated with fear again, and this fear disappears only slowly, even after I have heard Sheila's voice.

For a long time they talk softly in the other room, but I finally hear the door opening and closing again. The steps retreat, and the car starts quickly before the car door bangs shut, as if another person were in the vehicle.

When Henri comes back, he looks determined and serious, and he has a big stack of newspapers under his arm.

He puts them on the bed, and stroking my damp, wispy hair, he says:

"You're safe now, Ann Mary. No one can harm you any longer, for they thought they had killed you, and now they have been killed themselves."

"Who?" I say breathlessly.

His lips and eyes are narrow as with pain from struggling with an inner vision. Slowly, as if he were pronouncing these names for the last time before silence and oblivion take over, he says:

"'Anthony' returned. That must have been the helicopter we heard. But then Nora was already dead. She had taken poison. But when 'Anthony' got into an argument with Mustapha, who was just a flunkey and, therefore, uninformed as to your significance, and when they began shooting and one of them threw a hand grenade, the house collapsed over them up there—over the living and the dead…"

"And Dave?" I cry.

Henri looks at me for a second with a fixed gaze. Then he says with the shadow of a smile:

"Dave was just window dressing. He was visiting a girl. That was his salvation.—Here, take this.

Sheila left it for you to help you through the night!" he adds quickly, handing me Sheila's flask when he sees how I'm feeling.

It takes a few minutes before I can speak again.

"—My significance? What's that supposed to mean?" I whisper.

"All that will become clear once you see the papers," Henri answers. "Here they are, and now you can go ahead and read them. They are about two months old."

He picks out one of them with a large picture on the front page.

"And here is Ann Mary Holden if it's possible for you to recognize her again. Good night, call me if you need anything." He stops in the doorway for a moment and looks at me.

I sit up in bed. In my aching, trembling hands I hold the newspaper which has a picture of a girl with long, dark hair and heavy eyebrows, a turned up nose, and a chin and mouth that resemble mine.

I begin reading.

CHAPTER ELEVEN · *Recollection*

It's almost morning. The newspapers are lying in a heap on the bed. I've read them all, read them and seen the pictures of my father and myself and the yacht we were on. I've read the black headlines like thunderclouds on the horizon, pregnant with lightning—screaming letters and roaring print about a world on the brink of war, a war the likes of which no one has ever seen, a war more terrible than any thought or imagination conjure up—a war of hell!

I now know what has happened since the borders were closed in those days, diplomatic relations broken off, and all regular mail stopped because of the censure in a world on the verge of madness, where entire cities committed collective suicide and armies mutineered for fear. But I had to go a long way to arrive at that, and it's strangely distant and unreal as if it were a part of another world and another age.

The only thing that's very close and real—as close and real as the room in Henri's house where I'm lying—but in contrast to that filled with incomprehensible pain, is this: That I, Ann Mary Holden, daughter of professor Cecil Holden, who everyone thinks is a traitor to his country just as he and everyone else seem to take for granted that I'm dead—that this young woman lying here in an unknown place wrapped in a man's grotesque bathrobe—no matter how absolutely meaningless and incredible the thought may be—at this moment holds both world peace and the future in her hand. And that there's only one way to save it, the costliest, the most painful way, which I don't dare think of yet…

Time and again I must walk the long way up to that point to prepare myself as "La Isla"—and Henri—have prepared me.

And now I'm walking it again.

There's a large house just like on the bills I found in the room on the sea. That was where I used to live. I see my father's stocky figure with his stooped back, his intelligent head, and his hair already white. He comes and goes, just the way I myself come and go. We walk together arm in arm in the park when it gets dark, and only the large, illuminated windows of the house are visible among the trees.

But there's a time before that, an earlier time, when I'm just a couple of braids above a skimpy little dress and a pair of long, skinny legs, and when that same figure is holding my hand, only he is more erect, and his hair is still dark with just a little gray. We are standing in a park with lots of statues, almost like the one on that other bill in the room on the sea. But one of the statues looks like my mother, for she is dead, and it's her grave we are standing in front of. A short distance away there's a young man in uniform. He has stepped aside because he is weeping, and you are not allowed to weep when you're in uniform.

And then there's a time after that when we are standing in the park with the statues again. This time my brother is not along, for he is dead, and my father's hair is gray and his back has begun to curve, and I'm still just a big girl standing next to him in my black coat. I nestle close to him, promising him that I'll never deceive him but love him and be true to him forever. And there are evenings in the large house, the institute, which we have moved into now because my father has so many visitors. There are meetings all the time, and cars pull up in front of the house, and there are evenings when I'm all alone playing with my brother's toys, with his movie cameras and his little airplanes and his collection of stuffed animals; but dad always comes into my room after I've gone to bed and sits there holding my hand in his until I fall asleep. He comes without fail, except when he's up north in Alaska where it's all snow and ice. Later on I go with him up there, too. I go skiing, and we live in a large house made of dark wood. One year we stay there all winter long until spring comes and the snow melts and everything is terribly wet and cold so that I catch pneumonia. Dad sits by my bed until I'm well, even though there are still people at the door dropping off papers and drawings for him to look over and sign.

Eventually I grow up, and I begin to accompany my father everywhere. He calls me his "lady," and we see a lot of people and go to a lot of parties.

Most of the time, though, we are up north where we now live in another house, which is not nearly as cozy as the wooden house and where the panes flicker at night in the glow of light from this town of huge, windowless buildings where my father is supervising the work. Finally I also realize what it is my father is working on and why people making speeches in his honor call him "the nation's great son" and "the benefactor of mankind." My father is completing the experiments that have failed so many times and in so many countries, experiments that will mean incredible masses of energy that will never be exhausted but make the greatest and wildest dreams come true in the new centuries of technology, creating possibilities of life for new billions of people. It is then—when his experiments are almost completed—that he becomes ill. I take care of him, and he recovers, but he needs a vacation, and we take a long trip.

We visit England and France and Scandinavia, where my grandmother was born and where my father studied as a young man. Everywhere we go there are parties and people who want to meet him and who shower us with gifts. But it makes him tired, and when we have traveled through Germany and Switzerland and have seen Rome as well, we receive an invitation from one of my father's wealthy and famous colleagues, an Egyptian—he was the one who looked like a bottle with a big belly when we saw him for the first time outside of the opera in Rome. We receive an invitation to a long and leisurely voyage in the Mediterranean aboard his big yacht.

My suspicion was aroused for the first time when he gave me a necklace, a lovely necklace of dark red garnets, because I had a girlfriend, a daughter of one of my father's coworkers, who had a necklace like that, too. She had smuggled it in from Czechoslovakia when she and her family escaped from the dictatorship there.

But I didn't know what it was that caused this fear, and I said nothing to my father about it. I thought maybe it was just my imagination, and I didn't suspect anything that morning when, after a wonderful phosphorescent voyage, we were somewhere east of Cyprus and a friend of our host's landed on the water next to the yacht in a new type of helicopter and invited us to watch the schools of fish from above. I tried it myself, and it was fun and exciting; then it was my father's turn. There was only space enough for one person in the cabin in addition to the pilot.

I can see the whole thing before me the way it happened. My father had just started, and I was about to lie down in a deck chair when I suddenly noticed an enormous shadow under the water, like that of a whale. I stared, and a moment later the colossal, gray U-boat emerged from the sea, and the helicopter headed right for it.

I still didn't want to believe what I was seeing, but when my father—probably made unconscious with an injection—was lowered to the U-boat like a lifeless bundle, and when I saw in that same instant that the yacht's crew was armed and that the "colleague" was coming toward me—I grabbed a kind of lifesaver—a little inflatable boat with a tiny motor that they had shown us how to use—from a crate and jumped into the sea.

I acted instinctively, figuring they wouldn't dare shoot at me, but I did expect them to come after me. I just didn't think I could do anything else.

But suddenly I understood what devils they were and what a top secret operation I was witnessing —for I saw the helicopter returning to the yacht and picking up the "colleague," and I'm sure they meant to pick me up, too. Right after that the yacht exploded and sank with the crew and everything, and all the wreckage was carefully picked up by the helicopter.

There was a little white dot way out on the horizon, a sailboat, and the helicopter was so thorough in its efforts to eradicate all traces that, miserable with despair and nausea, I had reached the side of the boat before the helicopter came after me, hovering above me like a large, horrible insect.

I remember Michael, for he was the one who was aboard the sailboat, yelling into my ear through the infernal din of the rotors as he was pulling me on board:

"Miss Holden. I'm a secret service agent. Just call me Michael! I suspected that yacht even though we had checked out everything without your father's knowledge. I'm here on my own, and I'll do whatever I can for you."

At that moment a second helicopter approached, and he yelled at the top of his lungs: "I'd advise you to remain on deck. Otherwise the guys up there will think I'm alone and start shooting."

But the helicopters landed on the water, and when the pilot of the first one, whom I had been sitting next to an hour ago and who had kidnaped my father, climbed over the railing, I hurled a heavy tackle at him while shouting something terrible, I no longer remember what. He finally came on board with the blood running down his face, and when he grabbed hold of me, I hit him and tore myself away, falling with a throbbing pain in my arm. The last thing I remember is that I wanted to call out "Michael! Michael!" but my mouth was full of water.

—And yet I remember something else that happened later—but again it's as in another life and another age:

I can hardly speak, it's as if I'm very small. I have my arm in a sling, and a man is sitting across from me playing with a doll. Then he gives it to me and keeps asking me what its name is. I say "Miriam," because that was my doll's name when

I was a little girl. The man turns his head and looks at another man, and they nod to each other, and outside there are always dogs.

But later on I'm the one whose name is Miriam, and the man who is sitting across from me is "Anthony," and I gradually become bigger—it is he who gradually makes me bigger and older. He scolds me whenever I'm afraid of the dogs, but he doesn't send the dogs away. One day he lets me look at myself in a mirror, and I think my blond hair is beautiful. I ask for a lipstick because I want to make myself pretty for "Anthony," who has made me fall in love with him, more and more, so that I'll do anything he wants me to and, as a matter of fact, I do that one day (I know that now!), after we have arrived on "La Isla." After all, I was so afraid in the helicopter and in the cave where he hid me every night at first. But I wanted him to protect me, and I was happy when he came to visit me every day at the clinic where I was lying with my aching arm. Later on in the apartment I was happy, too—until, until he had to go away. There was also a film I couldn't stand to watch but ran away from. The sea roared louder than ever, but I finally woke up and was myself again that morning on "La Isla" where they kept me alive—why?

—"*Why*?" I say aloud.

An hour has passed. It must be quite light outside. Henri has had a visitor with a voice that could only be Michael's, and Michael has left again.

Once more I've said the word aloud, and Henri has come in. He opens up the shutters, letting the sun in and turning off the lamp, my vigil lamp, which he then carries out.

I get up for a moment, check the table, and find what I'm looking for. Then I lie down on the bed.

"Don't you know why?" he says when he comes in again. His eyes have that light blue closest to the pupils again, but they look strained and slightly red because he, too, has kept vigil, sitting up with me. A muscle twitches in his cheek.

"Oh yes, I know," I say slowly, seeking his eyes, which are suddenly unnaturally shiny—or is it mine? His face becomes a blur. I see only his eyes, and the light glistens and hurts my own—but even so I speak calmly and very slowly, letting him know that I've understood everything:

"The idea was to keep me alive so that they could bribe my father when the international tension had subsided. But they wanted to make out that I had drowned. It would be cause for war if it became common knowledge that they were holding me prisoner.—If I were found here with amnesia, nothing would happen. They could always dream up an explanation—a psychological problem, a disagreement with my father whom the entire world acknowledges as a traitor now that his voice and handwriting have been duplicated in statements in which he swears allegiance to the "people's democracies" of the East, and actors have imitated him on television if he himself wasn't hypnotized…"

"Yes, that's the way it is," Henri says softly.

"Do you think…do you think my father is working for them?" I almost can't get the words out.

"No," Henri says, sitting down and touching my shoulder for the first time. "You were the only one who could make him do that, and if that didn't work, they had installed a defective gas line in the apartment above yours. You know what I mean. Michael and Sheila have been busy tonight."

We are both silent for a while. I lean heavily on Henri.

"Yes, but 'Anthony,' when he is found? Won't they connect the two of us?" I shiver and squeeze Henri's arm.

"'Anthony' has been made unrecognizable, just as unrecognizable as that photographer who had the misfortune to show an interest in your house on the sea. I told you that Michael and Sheila have been busy."

I look inquisitively at Henri, and suddenly I feel a little prick in my arm. He smiles, showing me the syringe and drying the prick with a cotton ball moistened with alcohol.

"They are former colleagues—beside the fact that Michael is her brother-in-law. She was working on helping him after his sensational get-away, which was made public all over the world, even here. She figured he would show up here in disguise and stay with old Don Ramon.—But they both thought *you* were dead. It was not until the night you were on your way to meet Michael that the connection occurred to him, and he gave orders that under no circumstances were you to be seen with him."

"And Nora?" My eyelids are getting heavy.

"She was a notorious Soviet spy, wanted all over the world. Her face, her thick lips, the whole thing was the result of an operation. They identified her from a gunshot to her hip."

I remember the little sway she had when she walked, and the lines on her neck.

"She was in love with…," I say faintly.

"Yes, she was in love with 'Anthony,' whose real name was Greek. She made a real mistake and paid the price," Henri mutters.

I feel his hand on my forehead and am aware he is covering me with a blanket. My eyes are closed, but I know he is there observing me, and now I hear his voice:

"When you wake up, you'll meet Michael. I wish I could spare you that meeting, because in him you'll also meet your father and be asked the impossible."

"Give us time," I whisper. "Didn't you say that was the most important thing?"

My hand knows where he is. It finds his cheek and his forehead as he kneels silently by my bed—

And he will discover only too late that in my other hand I hold the ampoule he thinks he has given me…*but then perhaps he will know that I've already met Michael high above in a room in the yellow hotel by the harbor and that I'm standing with my face turned away as he leaves, beardless, transformed, and fossilized; and that afterward I'll be standing for a long time by the window looking out over "La Isla," which all of us here will leave behind one day without a name only to come into existence behind the barely visible horizons out there.*

I think about Blond Pete who is gone and wonder where he may be now. I wish I could speak one more time with Dave and Rebecca, who are walking down there by the harbor far from each other without knowing that I see them at this moment and that these tears that are turning the light into stars fill my eyes for their sake, now that I'm holding a hand in mine again, a hand that I mustn't tempt.

And I squeeze that hand until my own slackens its grip.

"Call me Miriam! *I whisper, for I'm on my way. I'm about to break out into the day...a little anonymous image, a doll...but no longer, no longer.*

GREEN INTEGER
Pataphysics and Pedantry

Douglas Messerli, *Publisher*

Essays, Manifestos, Statements, Speeches, Maxims,
Epistles, Diaristic Notes, Narratives, Natural Histories,
Poems, Plays, Performances, Ramblings, Revelations
and all such ephemera as may appear necessary
to bring society into a slight tremolo of confusion
and fright at least.

MASTERWORKS OF FICTION
Green Integer Books

Masterworks of Fiction is a program of Green Integer to
reprint important works of fiction from all centuries. We
make no claim to any superiority of these fictions over others
in either form or subject, but rather we contend that these
works are highly enjoyable to read and, more importantly,
have challenged the ideas and language of the times in which
they were published, establishing themselves over the years
as among the outstanding works of their period. By
republishing both well known and lesser recognized titles in
this series we hope to continue our mission bringing our
society into a slight tremolo of confusion and fright at least.

BOOKS IN THIS SERIES

José Donoso *Hell Has No Limits* (1966)

Knut Hamsun *A Wanderer Plays on Muted Strings* (1909)
Raymond Federman *The Twofold Vibration* (1982)
Gertrude Stein *To Do: A Book of Alphabets and Birthdays* (1957)
Gérard de Nerval *Aurélia* (1855)
Tereza Albues *Pedra Canga* (1987)
Sigurd Hoel *Meeting at the Milestone* (1947)
Leslie Scalapino *Defoe* (1994)
Charles Dickens *A Christmas Carol* (1843)
Michael Disend *Stomping the Goyim* (1969)
Anthony Powell *Venusberg* (1932)
Ole Sarvig *The Sea Below My Window* (1960)

*

Green Integer Books

Green Integer EL-E-PHANT Books (6 x 9 format)